SHORT-ORDER SHERIFF

RIver's End Ranch Book 1

KIRSTEN OSBOURNE

Unlimited Dreams

Introduction

Kelsi Weston, the youngest of six siblings, loves life. She has a job she adores, is surrounded by people she loves, and gets to work with people she cares about. If only she could keep cooks in the café she manages, life would be perfect. When her long-time boyfriend announces he's leaving town for a new job on the same day her cook leaves with no notice, she does what she always does. She handles it.

Sheriff Shane Clapper has loved Kelsi for years, going to her café for lunch every day simply so he can see her. When he hears she's broken up with her boyfriend, he immediately goes to the café to make his move. Why let grass grow under his feet? He knows what he wants, and he plans to get it! Will the sheriff be able to convince Kelsi she would be happier with him? Or will she give into her mother's demands to date the man picked out for her?

To sign up for Kirsten Osbourne's mailing list visit
kirstenandmorganna.com

Acknowledgments

I have to take this time to thank the woman who has agreed to keep up with all the storylines and make sure we mesh on this huge project I'm embarking on with my dear friends. Amy Petrowich, I don't know how you keep all those little details in your head, but someone has to, and I'm greatly impressed that you can! Thank you for taking on this project with us!

This book is the beginning of an awesome project with Pamela Kelly, Amelia Adams, Caroline Lee, and Cindy Caldwell. All of the books will be "sweet" romances, meaning there will be no explicit scenes, and they will all intertwine in the world of River's End Ranch that we've created. Every week for five weeks, starting on October 10th will be a new book. After that, it will be every other week. I encourage you to read all of the books for the full story of this amazing world I feel so honored to write in!

Every sibling will eventually find love as well as so many of the people you've already read about. Yes, all my worlds will collide as part of this ranch, because that's how my worlds seem to work. Thank you for following my journey! I appreciate each and every one of you.

Kirsten

Chapter One

KELSI WESTON LOOKED at her cook, Kathy, frustrated. "You can't leave us with no notice at all!" Why did all the cooks she hired take off so quickly? It made her crazy.

Kathy shrugged. "I have to. Did you see him?" She pointed to one of the guests of the dude ranch where Kelsey's Kafé was located, who was waiting for her at the front of the café. "He wants to take me away from all this and keep me in the style to which I want to become accustomed. Please understand!"

Kelsi looked at the guest with a frown. He was handsome, but a good fifteen years older than Kathy. Kelsi had no doubt that the real draw was his wallet and not his face. "How are we supposed to feed the guests that come in here?" Kelsi couldn't man both the front and the back.

"I'll work 'til noon. I don't really have to be packed until this evening, and I don't have much."

Kelsi sighed. Kathy had drifted in six months before looking for a job, so she wasn't terribly surprised she was drifting out the same way.

"I'll call Dani and see if she can fill in for the rest of

the week."Dani was Kelsi's twin, and she filled in whenever they were between cooks, which happened more often than Kelsi would like.

She saw her boyfriend, whom she'd been dating for eight years and annoyed with for most of that time, settle into a booth with a wave. Donn would have to wait, though, because she had to deal with her cook crisis first.

Kathy hugged Kelsi and ran out to tell her man that she would leave with him, but work that morning first.

Kelsi quickly dialed her sister's cell number, picturing her at her desk in the main ranch house. When Dani answered, she already sounded slightly peeved, and Kelsi put on her best happy voice. "How's my favorite sister?"

"Only sister. What do you need, Kelsi?"

Kelsi sighed. "How's your day?" She knew if she could get her sister to talk for a minute first, she'd be a lot less grumpy about her request.

"I'm working here. What do you need?" The annoyance in her twin's voice was getting stronger by the minute.

"Kathy is running off with one of the guests. I talked her into working until noon, but I'm going to need you to fill in," Kelsi finally just told her, sensing that her sister was going to be very difficult to deal with that day, even more so than usual.

Dani, short for Daniella, groaned. "Why can't you keep a cook in that café? I don't understand the problem."

"I wish I could answer that! I can't cook *and* manage the front *and* wait tables. You know that's too much for one person. Please, Dani! We can't shut the café down or Mom and Dad will hear about it and kill us!"

Their parents hadn't yet passed the ranch down to their six offspring, and it felt like they never would. Their mother had mentioned some sort of test for them, but Kelsi didn't know what it was yet. She wasn't sure she wanted to. For now, she knew their parents had spies in town, and they needed to keep everything running as smoothly as possible.

The six siblings had been raised as a tight-knit unit, along with their cousin Jess, who'd come to live with them when she was eight. Their grandparents had a house there on the property as well, and they had all spent a great deal of time together—for good and for bad.

"I'll be there. Just make sure I don't have to come out of the kitchen and deal with any people. People are not my friends, and they are not to be brought back into the kitchen to meet the chef, or any of that quirky nonsense you like to pull. Not today, and not ever. Got it?"

Kelsi sighed with relief. "Got it. Dani owns the kitchen, and Kelsi owns the front. No people for Dani, because all are evil and must be destroyed. Please don't poison anyone, Dani! Please!" She couldn't help teasing her sister because, well, she was fun to tease!

"Done listening to you!"

Kelsi looked down at the phone in her hand. Her sister had ended the call. She smiled happily, bouncing over to where Donn sat in a booth waiting for her. "Hey, you."

Donn hadn't been by in over a week, and he hadn't called much, but that's just how he was. Kelsi wasn't terribly worried. She was busy with her own life, and wasn't exactly waiting for Donn to put a ring on it. "We need to talk."

"So talk." She looked around, glad it was during the lull between breakfast and lunch, the only two meals the café was open for. Most of the guests ate their dinner in the restaurant that was part of the main ranch house. Some cooked for themselves or meandered into town. In May they would start offering chuck wagon meals for dinner, and a lot of the guests would like that.

"I'm moving to California."

Kelsi blinked at him a couple of times. "Really? Why?" She wasn't hurt by his announcement at all, which told her how bad their relationship had become. He was like a well-worn shoe. She was used to him, but not in love. She wasn't sure she'd ever been in love. It was always good to have a man around for dress-up events or for the odd Saturday night, though.

"I got a job at Disneyland. Being that close to Hollywood, I'm sure someone will spot me, and I'll get the big break I've been waiting for."

"Really?" Donn had always thought he was a gifted actor and incredibly handsome, and she was sure he was in his own mind. "What about your job here on the ranch?" He did a lot of the maintenance work at River's End Ranch, the dude ranch she and her siblings ran under their parents' watchful gaze, wherever they happened to be at the moment.

"I'll go tell the boss," he said, referring to her brother, Wade, the ranch's general manager. There were six siblings in all, and they all played essential roles in keeping the ranch going, now that their parents were off exploring North America in a Winnebago.

"When will you leave?" she asked curiously. "And what are you going to do at Disney?"

"Well, I'm hoping eventually I'll get one of the prince roles, but right now, I'm going to be selling cotton candy in one of those little carts."

She wanted to laugh at him and tell him he was an idiot, but truly, she didn't care enough. "When are you leaving?"

"This afternoon. I found a guy to room with, and I'm heading out. My car is all packed, but I thought you'd want to know."

"Yeah, it's usually a good idea to let your girlfriend of eight years know when you're about to move out of town and leave the job her family has given you. I appreciate the head's up." *Two people quitting without notice in one day must be a record. I hope Mom and Dad don't hear about this.*

"Don't be ugly about this, Kelsi. You knew the job was temporary."

Kelsi shrugged. "I'm really *not* being ugly. I wish you the best."

"You should come down and see me soon."

"Why would I do that?" she asked. It was early April, and the snow was mostly melted. She was ready for the summer tourist crowds the ranch brought. Kelsi loved her home in Idaho more than she could ever express. If he didn't, he was welcome to move on.

"Because you're my girl?"

She laughed. "I don't think I've really been your girl since a month or two after graduation. Goodbye, Donn. I hope you have a good life." She stood and walked toward the back of the café to the kitchen, proud of her calm, dignified exit, until she tripped over a box and slammed into the wall. So much for being dignified. She didn't care though. She was glad to wash her hands of him.

* * *

Sheriff Shane Clapper, the chief of all law enforcement in Riston, Idaho, sat down at his desk and looked at the paperwork that had been piled there while he was out on patrol that morning. He was already looking forward to going down to Kelsey's Kafé for lunch. He loved to watch Kelsi Weston in action. She could charm an entire café full of ranchers and cops and guests in five minutes flat. It was the highlight of his day, most days.

5

One of the three deputies that worked under him, Bartholomew Bigelow, wandered in from the kitchen, a donut in one hand and a cup of coffee in the other. "Hey, Sheriff."

"Must you be so stereotypical?" Shane mumbled under his breath. "Anything going on in town?"

Bart sat on the edge of his own desk to answer. "No crimes or anything to report. But rumor has it that Donn Samuels left town pulling a U-Haul trailer behind his truck."

Shane felt his breath catch for a moment. "Really? Any idea where he's going?" Did that mean Kelsi was finally free of the idiot?

Bart shook his head. "Nope, but I bet you aim to find out."

Most people in town knew how Shane felt about little Kelsi Weston, except maybe the woman herself. "I think I may have to go over there and get myself a cup of coffee right now. Paperwork can wait." He wasn't sure he'd have been able to remain at a crime scene with the news he'd just been given. It was like a giant magnet was pulling him toward the River's End Ranch and Kelsey's Kafé.

He stood and put his hat on his head, striding toward the door. If Kelsi was available, he wasn't going to wait for her to find someone else. No, this was his chance with the sweet woman, and she was going to be his.

Once he was in his car, he seriously considered turning his lights on to get to the café as quickly as he could, but he was sure someone would spot him and follow him. People in Riston didn't have the kind of respect for the law he would like to see, because they were just a bit too curious about whatever crime could be taking place. It was different where he'd come from. He loved the town too much to complain about it a lot, but he did frequently warn its citizens to wait in their cars if he was approaching with his siren blaring. Of course, sirens were usually only used for traffic stops in Riston.

Ten minutes later, without the use of his lights and sirens, he pulled up in front of the café and went inside, nabbing one of the corner booths. It was after eleven, so he could order his lunch and take his time with it.

He didn't have to wait long for Kelsi to come and see about him. She was wearing a pair of black slacks and a bright pink top under her apron. Her hips swayed as she walked to the booth and sat down across from him instead of standing to take his order. "You're early today, Sheriff. Did you forget to eat your Frosted Flakes before heading to work?"

Shane grinned. "Nope. I heard tell of a certain idiot leaving town pulling a U-Haul, and I thought I'd come find out for myself what the story is." He was never one to beat around the bush. After ten years of law enforcement, there didn't seem to be a reason.

Kelsi shrugged one slender shoulder, her ice blue eyes meeting his. "If you're talking about my idiot ex-boyfriend, Donn, he decided he was going to give up his job here at the ranch, with no notice, to go and make cotton candy at Disneyland. He's going to get discovered by some big Hollywood producer there, or maybe he'll be one of the Disney princes. He's not sure yet."

Shane looked at her carefully. "You don't seem too broken up about it."

"I'm not. We should have broken up years ago." She pushed her blond hair out of her eyes. "He wasn't right for me. Never has been."

"Why did you date him for so long then?"

She shrugged again, her eyes intense. "Habit, I guess. He asked me out in our junior year of high school, and it seemed like more effort than it was worth to break up with him. Besides, it was always good to have a date for weddings."

"So how long do you think a man should wait after a girl he's had his eye on breaks up with her boyfriend of eight years? Is there a set amount of time that's best?"

Kelsi looked at Shane, with his dark brown hair and eyes of chocolate brown. She hadn't thought of him as potential boyfriend material, because she'd been part of a couple for so long, but now that she considered it, the idea seemed like a good one. "Oh, I don't know. Depends on the man who's wanting to know."

"What if it's me who wants to know?"

"Let me think about it." She tilted her head to one side, tapping her index finger on one cheek. "I think maybe ten minutes is a long enough wait." She had little butterflies in her belly at the idea of going out with him, but she'd play it cool. It was never good to give a man too much power in a relationship from what she'd read.

"That does seem sufficient, doesn't it?"

"Well, it's not like you're asking me to marry you." Although that idea was intriguing as well. She wondered if a child of theirs would have his dark looks or her eyes like blue ice?

"Well, I considered it, but thought it might be better if I took you to a movie first." He winked at her, doing his best not to let on just what he was feeling. Kelsi was his dream girl, and everything he'd ever wanted in a woman. He needed to take things nice and slow so she wouldn't be scared away.

"A movie? It would be nice if we had a theater in Riston, wouldn't it?"

"I could go to the Redbox at the drugstore in town and rent a DVD. I wouldn't mind watching it in the living room of the ranch house, or you could come to my place and watch it." He'd rather she came to his place, of course, but he knew she was careful about her reputation.

"We'd better keep it in the guest living room of the ranch house if you don't want my brothers coming down on you." Kelsi's four older brothers could be a pain, but she loved them all. "You know how they get."

Shane nodded. "I'd hope they'd trust the sheriff, but I know them, and I'm sure they don't." They were stereotypical older brothers where she and Dani were concerned.

She laughed softly. "When are we going to watch this movie?"

"Well, I know it's Monday night, but I'm not waiting for Friday or Saturday, so let's say tonight. Do you have a preference on the movie?"

Kelsi shrugged. "Something gruesome."

He shook his head at her. "So the rumors are true, are they?" He'd made a habit of gathering as much information about Kelsi as possible over the years, knowing it would only help when he finally had his chance with her.

"What rumors?" Kelsi asked, a grin playing at her lips.

"The rumors that you only like movies if there's enough blood to drown somebody in."

"I have a unique taste in films. What can I say?" She'd always loved the teen horror films, filled with blood and gore. They were great date movies when she was in her teens, because she could bury her face against the shoulder of her escort whenever she wanted.

He frowned. "Maybe you should provide the movie. I'm not sure Redbox is going to run to slasher movies."

"Okay! I've got a nice collection of DVDs to choose from. We'll pick when you get there." Her mind was already going through the collection. She'd have five ready

9

for him to choose from. Hopefully there would be one or two he hadn't had the pleasure of watching yet.

"I'm off at five. We could do dinner in the restaurant at six? Can you get us in?"

Kelsi nodded. "Sounds good to me, and I can always get us in." She had always had fun with Shane and looked forward to an evening with him. He may be as much of a dud as Donn had turned out to be, but she'd never know unless she went out with him.

Dani walked in through the front door then, surprising Kelsi. "I figured you'd sneak in the back so no one would know you were here!" Kelsi called to her sister.

Dani wrinkled her nose at her identical twin. "Yeah, well I didn't see any cars but the sheriff's, so I figured we were safe. I can't work this Saturday, so you'd better have a replacement for me by then. I have to do my search and rescue training." She folded her arms over her chest as if daring her sister to have a problem with it.

Kelsi frowned. "Who am I going to get on short notice?" She looked over at Shane, a twinkle in her eye. "You've filled in before in a pinch."

Shane nodded. "Yeah, I'll be here if you need me."

"I will." She scooted out of the booth. "What can I get you for lunch, Sheriff?"

"Burger and fries. Chocolate shake." He wasn't sure if Kelsi even realized she'd never brought him a menu, but it didn't really matter. He had their menu memorized right down to the daily specials. He wasn't fond of the chicken and dumplings they made on Mondays, so he chose from one of the regular offerings.

"Coming right up."

He caught her hand as she went to hurry away. "I'm really looking forward to tonight."

She smiled down at him, her heart racing at his touch.

Had it ever done that with Donn? She wasn't sure. She knew it hadn't in years. "I am too."

She followed her sister into the kitchen and gave the order. As soon as Kathy saw Dani, she flung her arms wide. "I'm free! No more slinging hash for me! I'll live in the lap of luxury now!"

Kelsi rolled her eyes. "Sure you will, Kathy. Sure you will." There had been a lot of cooks over the years who had run off with different guests of the ranch. Most had requested their jobs back, but if they hadn't given a proper notice, they hadn't gotten them.

Kathy threw her arms around Dani, who pushed her away. Refusing to be thwarted, Kathy rushed to Kelsi and hugged her tight. "Be happy for me!"

"How 'bout if I'm happy for you and annoyed for me?" Kelsi asked.

"That works!" Kathy untied her apron and dropped it on the counter. "Bye! Thanks for all the fun." She rushed out of the café, leaving the sisters in the kitchen.

Kelsi smiled at Dani. "We get to work together for a while again. I know—this time, you call me Louise, and I'll call you Thelma! They'll be our fun secret names for each other!" She always tried to add more fun into her work, and she loved to tease and try to coerce Dani into joining in with her nonsense.

Dani raised an eyebrow at her twin. "Don't think I don't remember that you named your breasts Thelma and Louise when we were twelve. No way am I going by the name of one of your boobs. Just call me Dani." She pulled on a clean apron. "I need you to whack off my hair again. Can you do it tonight?"

Kelsi shook her head. "I have a date."

"Donn The Dweeb coming over again?"

"Nope. Donn was yesterday's news. He's on his way to

sunny California to make cotton candy for Disney and sell it from one of those little carts. I'm going out with the sexy sheriff tonight." Kelsi wiggled her eyebrows at her sister.

Dani raised an eyebrow at her sister. "Shane? He's been hot for you forever. It's about time you gave him a chance."

"You think?"

Dani laughed. "I know. The whole town knew. You're so oblivious sometimes, Kelsi."

"Don't you mean Louise?"

Dani's face shut down. "What's the sheriff having for lunch?"

*** * ***

Kelsi dug through her closet frantically that afternoon, trying to find just the right thing to wear for her date with Shane. She wanted to be casual, but elegant. She found a pair of jeans and a cute top that would be just right, but the only shoes she had that went well with the outfit pinched her toes.

She hurried to the room next door to hers and knocked. "I need shoes!" she called through the closed door, before opening it without getting a response.

"Go away!" Dani said as Kelsi barged into her room, heading straight for her closet.

"What's the point of having a sister the exact same size as you if you can't borrow her clothes?" Kelsi asked, already looking through the shoe options available to her.

"I don't think there is a point to having an identical twin. I haven't figured one out yet at least."

"Why are you always so grumpy?" Kelsi asked, finding a pair of red cowboy boots. "Can I wear these?"

"What if I say no? Will you listen to me?"

"Of course not! Thanks, Dani, you're the best!" Kelsi rushed out of her sister's room shutting the door behind her, and then hurrying back to open it.

"Yes?"

"I'll cut your hair tomorrow night if you don't want to go to the spa to have it done."

"Why would I go to the spa and pay some stranger to run their fingers through my hair when you'll do it for free?"

"I love you, Dani!"

"Uh huh." Dani kept reading her book, not even looking up as her sister closed her door and hurried away.

By six, Kelsi was ready for her date with Shane. She wore the jeans, a red sweater that hugged her curves, and her sister's cowboy boots. She had made reservations at the restaurant, annoying the staff to no end, because there was no room for her, and picked out the movie choices she wanted to give Shane.

Because the house she shared with her sister was also the main house of the family's dude ranch, Shane walked right in without knocking, the same way everyone in town did. They'd decorated it to look like a home, but there were little touches that made it obvious it was a business.

She found Shane in the library waiting for her. "Hey, you're here already. Sorry, I would have come out sooner if I'd known."

He stood up from one of the overstuffed chairs, placed there for the guests to read in.

"I don't mind waiting a minute or two for you." He looked her up and down, his eyes appreciative. "You look fabulous."

Kelsi did a little spin, letting him see the full effect of her outfit. She'd fixed her hair instead of pulling it back into the ponytail she always wore for work, and she felt pretty for a change.

"We have reservations at the restaurant."

He held out his hand, letting her know to precede him into the hallway. "Thanks for making the reservations happen. I'm sure I wouldn't have been able to get in."

The restaurant at the ranch house was used not only for the dude ranch guests, but it was also the most popular restaurant in town. It was only open for dinner, and you had to book a couple of weeks in advance if you wanted to eat there—unless you were family, of course. They warned every guest who called to reserve a room to book their meals in the restaurant as soon as they could, so they wouldn't miss being able to eat there.

Shane wore a pair of jeans with a button up shirt and his favorite cowboy hat. "I love your boots."

She grinned. "I borrowed them from Dani, despite her protests."

He laughed, knowing how the twins' relationship worked. "They look really good on you."

"I think so," she said with a wink.

Shane watched her as they walked through the house and waited to be seated. He'd lived in Riston for ten years, since she was about fourteen. He'd moved there at eighteen to start his career in law enforcement, and had quickly been elected sheriff. He'd known her the entire time, but she hadn't really caught his eye until four years before. Her fun, quirky personality had drawn her to him, though her slender figure and pretty face hadn't hurt.

"What time do you need me at the café Saturday?" he asked, not wanting to talk business, but figured he'd get it over with, and they'd move on.

"Five? People start coming in about five-thirty for breakfast."

He groaned softly. "You know how much I hate mornings, right?"

She grinned at him. "I'll make the coffee extra strong for you."

"You're the best."

Chapter Two

_____

ONCE THEY WERE SEATED at a table right outside the kitchen Shane was sure wasn't usually there, he looked around. "You know I don't think I've ever actually brought a date here before." He'd been to the restaurant once or twice, but not often. He enjoyed cooking enough that he usually made himself dinner.

His name had never been attached to anyone else's that Kelsi knew of, so she shrugged. "Sometimes it's easier to just drive into Boise for a date."

"Or make them dinner at my place." He looked at her over his menu. "I'd like to cook for you sometime." It was weird taking her to a restaurant that was attached to the back of her home. Yes, it was the nicest restaurant in town, but it was still strange.

"That would be nice. I mean, I've eaten your cooking because you cook for the café on occasion, but it would be nice to eat something you'd cooked special for me." She took a sip of the water in front of her. "I can cook too, you know." She didn't like it much, but she could do it and do it well.

He raised an eyebrow at that. "Really? Why don't you ever cook and let Dani work out front?"

She rolled her eyes. "Can you see letting Dani deal with the guests? No, she's the Weston we keep behind closed doors where she can't run anyone off." Her sister's grumpy moods were legendary around Riston.

"She's not that bad!" he protested, not really meaning it. Dani was downright scary when she was in a mood, and he avoided her as much as possible. He preferred her sweet-tempered twin.

"She actually threw an egg at my head today, because a customer complained that his burger was too rare." Kelsi sighed. "I don't know what we're going to do with her, but I know I love her."

"I've never seen identical twins who were more different! Your hair isn't even the same color."

She grinned. "Dani's is natural, and I give mine a little boost in the blond department." Dani had the mousy brown hair that was natural to both of them, but Kelsi felt it was too lackluster. She wanted the blond to match her personality.

He shook his head. "And hers is always so short, and looks like someone took a hatchet to it."

"Well, that's because she keeps coming to me for haircuts, and I have no clue what I'm doing. I think she wants to look as different from me as possible. Mom always made us dress alike when we were little, because she was so excited to have mono-zygotic twins."

He blinked a few times. "Mono-zygotic, huh?"

She wrinkled her nose. "Sometimes it's fun to use the real names for stuff."

The waiter, Steve, stopped by to take their orders then. "Hi, Kelsi. Sheriff. What can I get you?"

Once they'd ordered, he wandered off. Kelsi knew

Steve was working his way through school in their restaurant, and he wouldn't be there forever, but she liked him.

"So tell me about you," Kelsi said. "I know you've been here for about ten years, but I have no idea where you came from. You just showed up one day, and you've been part of the town ever since."

He sipped his water, watching her closely. "I grew up in Southern California, and hated the constant temperatures. I wanted real seasons. I know everyone is supposed to love it there, but I didn't. I moved here right after high school, because I saw an ad for a deputy on a job search site. As soon as I got here, I felt like I was home."

"You have a house in town, right?" she asked, just then realizing she had no idea where he lived. The ranch was so huge that it was almost entirely self-contained. She had no need to go into town often, because she ordered everything she wanted from Amazon. She was constantly surrounded by people, living in what was basically a hotel, so there was never a need to go search out companionship.

"Yeah, I live on Main Street. You know the white house with the blue shutters next door to the bowling alley? That's mine."

"I know exactly which house you mean!" She took another sip of her water as the waiter put their food on the table. "So tell me something, Sheriff?"

"Anything." He had nothing to hide from her. He liked that she was asking questions.

"What's a big, sexy sheriff like you doing still single?"

Shane laughed, shaking his head. "You're not afraid to say anything, are you?"

Kelsi shrugged. "Should I be?" She believed in speaking her mind and asking what she wanted to know. How else would she get to know him better?

"Not at all." He cut a bite off his steak, spearing it with

his fork. "I've been waiting for you to realize you were dating a loser, so I could ask you out."

She laughed. "Sure you have. Seriously, why haven't you dated anyone? We have so many women in and out of the ranch, I'd have expected you to be dating regularly."

"I'm not kidding. I've been waiting for you." He ate the bite of his steak, chewing it slowly, and following it up with a sip of water. "You caught my eye about four years ago, and I've been biding my time ever since."

"Why didn't you say something?" If she'd known he was hanging around, she might have done something about Donn. Of course, she'd barely known him four years before, so maybe not.

He shrugged. "You seemed to be happy, and I wasn't going to be the reason you broke it off with your high school sweetheart."

"I am happy. I always have been. Happiness is so much more than the romantic relationship you're in. Happiness is waking up every morning in the middle of the most beautiful piece of land God put on this earth. Happiness is knowing my family loves me and will do anything for me— even if they're grumpy about it. Happiness is being Kelsi Weston and doing the job I love every single day. No man can take that from me."

He nodded, raising his water glass to her. "To Kelsi Weston, the strongest, happiest woman I know. And the most beautiful."

She blushed but raised her glass to clink against his. "Beauty fades. Strength lasts forever."

"So tell me about the history of River's End Ranch. I'm dying to know. There are so many stories around town about your family—one has a gunslinger moving into town and killing off the people who lived in the house—making it his own. Another says that one of your ancestors moved here during the latter half of the nineteenth century, along with a brother, and one of them ordered a bride from back east somewhere. Just all kinds of weird stuff."

She smiled. "Alas, there is no gunslinger in my family's history, so I have to say that didn't happen. The second story is mostly true. A brother and a sister came out here to homestead, each choosing a different section of land. The sister pretended to be a man when she signed for her part of the land, and she got herself a mail order groom from the east. The brother died young, unmarried, but not until after he'd "proved up" the land, so the sister inherited that. The two of them had a couple of kids and all worked hard, starting a ranch. They gradually bought up the homesteads of others around them. By the 1940s, all the land that's part of River's End Ranch was here. It was huge. My great-grandmother had in her head that it would be nice to have a hotel on the land, and the dude ranch part of the business was born. We still run cattle to entertain the guests, but the biggest part of our business is tourism now."

Shane smiled, nodding. "That's fascinating. Could women not homestead?"

Kelsi shook her head vehemently. "They were still men's property during that time. Don't get me started on that bit of nonsense!" Every time she thought about the story, she wanted to travel back in time with a gun and show the authorities what a woman could do.

"What about the café? Did your great-grandparents start the café too?"

"That was all Grandma Kelsey, who married Granddad Wilfred. Grandma Kelsey wanted there to be a place for guests to eat during the day that didn't include her cooking, so she started Kelsey's Kafé. She hated to cook, but it's her recipes we still serve. She was a lot like me, as she enjoyed visiting with customers and waiting tables, and I remember going there to work with her when I was little. She died when I was sixteen, but she taught me so much about life, love, and the restaurant business. I always knew it would be my place to take over."

"Sounds like you loved her," Shane said, pushing his plate away.

"I have so many happy memories of working with her waiting tables in the café. I know that's got to sound crazy, but I love this whole place more than I've ever loved a person. It's home."

He nodded. "I felt the same thing the first time I set foot in Riston. It was like this was the place I'd been searching for my whole life. My dad was a Silicon Valley guy, so he really doesn't get Idaho or the whole law enforcement thing, but I'm doing what I was called to do."

"It was so weird to me that Donn spent so much time trying to find ways to leave Riston. This is my little version of heaven on earth, and he hated it. He complained every day that he needed to find a way to make his dreams come true and that it was awful here. He hated the winters." She sighed. "I love the winters. Of course, I'm all excited now because winter's almost over and the snow is melting and the tourist season is about to get into full swing."

"How do you feel about summer and fall?" he asked, a twinkle in his eye.

"Summer brings swimming and boating and all the fun things that you can do on a ranch. And fall means the leaves are changing colors and soon we'll be able to have our first snowfall and Christmas and snowmobiling." She shrugged. "I told you I love Idaho. I love *all* the seasons!"

"I'm glad, because I can't imagine ever wanting to leave this place." And he had a feeling that before too terribly long, he'd be willing to do just about anything she asked.

Steve stopped at the table then. "Are you guys getting dessert?" he asked.

Shane looked at Kelsi. "You want dessert?"

"Yeah, I want dessert, but I want to take it to the living room. We're going to watch some blood and gore." Her whole face gave away her excitement as she looked up at Steve and announced their plans.

Steve flinched. "I'll make sure to stay away from the living room on my way out tonight. I don't know how you can watch that crap!"

"It's a learned taste. One you should work on learning immediately! How will you ever teach your children to love blood and guts?"

"I'm not married. No kids on the way. What do you want for dessert?"

Kelsi grinned. "I'll take some huckleberry pie, please!" She got the same dessert every time. Why would she waste calories on an inferior dessert?

Shane looked at her. "Huckleberry pie? I know it's supposed to be an Idaho thing, but is it really any good?" He'd never tried it, even though he almost felt guilty for it. Huckleberry pie was practically synonymous with Idaho.

She blinked at him. "A piece of warm huckleberry pie with a single scoop of vanilla ice cream is worth fighting a battle for. I promise if you order it and don't like it, I'll finish it for you!"

"You're so kind. So why don't I order a different dessert and have one bite of yours?"

"You want a bite of my pie?" Kelsi frowned for a moment. "Fine, but when you realize I got the better dessert, you still don't get to eat mine."

Shane shrugged. "Whatever. I can live with that." He

turned to Steve who was waiting patiently, obviously used to Kelsi. "I'll have the cheesecake with caramel sauce please."

As Steve walked off, Kelsi leaned forward as if to impart a great secret. "You've been out-ordered."

He laughed. "Everything is a competition with you, Kelsi."

"How many siblings do you have?"

He wasn't sure what that had to do with anything, but answered anyway, "I have a sister who is five years younger than me."

"Aha!" she said triumphantly.

"Aha? What does that mean?" He felt like she was speaking in riddles.

"That's why you think I'm competitive. You didn't have five siblings breathing down your neck playing Monopoly, Yahtzee, and every other game known to man! You didn't have a twin you were trying to walk faster than! You didn't have to worry about who lost all their teeth first, because you always knew it would be you. Me? I wasn't noticed unless I was the best at something! So...I'm the best darn waitress and café manager in my whole family!"

Her brother, Will, walked up to the table. "Dani said you finally dumped Donn The Dork." He was looking back and forth between her and Shane as if he wanted to say something.

"Hi, Will. It's so good to see you! It's been ages!" Kelsi said with a smile, wishing he'd go away. Her brother Will was her favorite and the one who frustrated her the most, all at once.

"I know! Since our weekly Sunday night dinner last night when you stole the last piece of huckleberry pie from me. I think your exact words were, 'You touch my pie and you draw back a bloody nub, and you know I'll do it!'

Weren't those your words?" He turned his attention to Shane. "And if it isn't the sheriff who's had the hots for my baby sister forever. Not letting any grass grow before you move in now that Donn The Dingleberry has moved away?"

Shane met her brother's eyes. "Would you?"

Will shrugged. "Probably not, but then, I'm not moving in on your little sister."

"Is this the big speech, warning me to be kind and loving and not take advantage of her, from all of you? Or can I expect three more visits along the same lines?" Shane wasn't going to back down. He was doing nothing wrong. Taking a woman in her mid-twenties to dinner in a public place was not a crime in any law book he'd ever read.

"Oh, we wouldn't want to deprive you! You'll talk to all four of us within the week, I'm sure. We're not committing crimes, Sheriff. Just making sure you know how precious our baby sister is to us."

Kelsi had heard enough. "Hey, Will, oh favorite brother-of-mine?"

"Yes, Kelsi?"

"Back off! I'm twenty-four and can handle myself. I've been doing it for years, so go away!" Kelsi's face was more determined than Shane had ever seen it.

Steve walked toward their table with the two desserts, but when he saw Will, he turned and walked straight back to the kitchen. Shane frowned as he watched.

Will glared down at Kelsi. "I'm your big brother. It's my job to make sure men in your life treat you with the respect you deserve."

Kelsi got to her feet, her short frame looking tiny in comparison to her brother's huge bulk. She went toe to toe with him, her neck cranked back so far it looked to Shane like it would hurt. He leaned back in his chair to watch the show.

She stabbed her finger into the middle of Will's chest. "I will fight my own battles, and I will make my own mistakes. You will back off and take all our muscle-bound idiot brothers with you! I'm not putting up with this for another minute. Do you hear me? I will make your life miserable if you keep this up, Will Weston! I'm not afraid of any of you, and I know all the right stuff to mix into your food to have you sitting in the bathroom for three months, because Grandma Kelsey taught me. Remember?"

Will took a step back, amazing Shane. Had she really just backed her brother up that way? He needed some popcorn, because this show was better than any movie.

Steve came back toward the table. "I'm going to call Wade to come kick you both out if you don't keep your voices down!" he hissed at the siblings. He carried two pieces of pie and a piece of cheesecake. He shoved one piece of pie at Will. "Go eat that and sweeten up your mood." The other piece of pie was put in Kelsi's hands. "Your bill is on your account. Go watch your slasher movie." He handed the cheesecake to Shane. "Get her out of here."

Shane blinked a few times, surprised an employee of the ranch would talk to two family members that way. He stood, throwing enough cash on the table for a tip, knowing he needed to get her out of the restaurant fast. He could feel the eyes of everyone in the room staring at them.

Will turned and walked away with his pie in hand, leaving the restaurant entirely.

Shane took Kelsi's arm and pulled her from the restaurant, his pie and a fork in his other hand. "I want you to tell me what they charge you for the meal, because it's my treat, not yours."

"Don't be ridiculous. It's my family's business. And Will may be my favorite brother, but I'm going to kill him if he tries to interfere with my life. I will poison him. I will slit his throat in his sleep. I will blow up his car!"

Shane shook his head. "Now if something happens to him, you'll be the first suspect! You don't make death threats to the local sheriff. What are you thinking!"

"Oh, you know as well as I do I wouldn't really kill him. I'll just make him very uncomfortable for a very long time."

Shane shook his head as he pulled her toward the family living room. How had he so quickly become embroiled in one of the famous fights between the Weston siblings? They were all known for their hot tempers and loyalty toward one another. They could say whatever they wanted to each other, but let an outsider even look at one of them funny, and the whole clan would descend on them, en masse.

He pulled her into the living room, a room that was for both family and guests, and was relieved to see it was empty. "Sit down and eat your pie. Where are the movies you picked for me to choose from?" He wanted her temper to calm before they moved much further, and he was sure pie was the answer. With Kelsi, there always seemed to be a sweet answer to everything. She treated chocolate as if it was medicinal.

She sat brooding as she watched him dig through the movies on the end table beside the couch. He chose one, *Student Bodies*, a spoof on the slasher movies of the seventies, and stuck it into the DVD player, before sitting down beside her with remote in hand.

"Now, where's my bite of huckleberry pie?" he asked,

looking at her and reaching out to rub a bit of huckleberry from the corner of her mouth with his thumb. He popped the thumb into his mouth, licking it clean. "Pretty good."

Kelsi was surprised by how much she wanted to kiss him. Instead, she scooped up a bite of the pie with her fork and fed it to him, watching his eyes close as he chewed. "You're right. You out-ordered me."

"I know," she said, taking another bite of pie for herself.

"Can we get another pie sent in here?"

Kelsi laughed. "The kitchen won't be doing any favors for Will *or* me tonight. They hate when we fight in the restaurant. The chef says it puts people off their food, and we Westons should stay away completely."

Shane was glad she was laughing again. "Okay, tell me about this movie we're about to watch." He was sitting at the end of the couch, and she was in the middle, sitting close to him. She pulled a quilt from the back of the couch and covered them both with it, moving a bit closer to him.

"It's one of my favorites. It's really a spoof on all the other slasher films. You're going to *love* the breather!"

"The breather?" he asked.

"Just watch. I can't tell you about it or you won't want to watch it!"

He started the movie and finished his cheesecake, putting his arm around her shoulders after he'd set the cheesecake plate on the table. He drew Kelsi closer and felt her rest her head on his shoulder, and he sighed content-edly. Happiness may be ranch and family to her, but to him, it was finally being able to date her and have the right to put his arm around her.

He watched her more than he watched the movie. She buried her face in the blanket or turned her face into his shoulder during the scary parts, which surprised him. He knew she'd probably seen the movie a bunch of times. The third time she hid her face, he paused the DVD.

"Why are you scared? I thought you'd seen this?"

Kelsi frowned up at him for a moment, wondering if she should just tell him the truth or pretend it was something else. Finally, she shrugged, deciding the truth was the easiest. "If I pretend I'm scared, I get to touch you more and bury my face in your shoulder. If I act all blasé like I've seen it a million times, which I have, I can't pretend to need comfort from you."

He blinked a couple of times in surprise at her honesty. "So you're using the scary movie as an excuse to get closer to me?"

She shrugged. "It's working, right?"

He laughed softly. "Does that mean you want me to kiss you?"

"I wouldn't have gone out with you if I didn't." Kelsi believed in honesty above all else. A little subterfuge was fine and dandy, but outright lies weren't her style.

He turned toward her. "Now? Cuz I can kiss you now. Or I can wait." He was nervous, and it surprised him. He'd spent so long thinking about her that actually touching her was nerve-wracking for him.

She grinned at him. "Here's how I see it. We don't know how strong our attraction really is until we kiss. I mean, we can think we'll have all this electricity between us, but kiss and find out we're just meant to be friends forever. Or we can kiss, and there could be magic. We need to see if we have the magic to know if we should go out again, so I think we should kiss now. Get it over with. You know?"

"Get it over with? You want to get our first kiss *over with*?" Shane shook his head. "This night just keeps getting more and more romantic."

"The fight with my brother was pretty great…and the movie is awesome, of course…but yeah, I'm not so good with romance. I do memorable *really* well, though!"

"You do have a point there. I don't think I could forget tonight if I tried." He sighed. "All right. Let's get the first kiss over with, but if it's not perfect, it's because I feel put on the spot, so then I get a do-over."

"You're already making excuses and asking for a do-over?" She rolled her eyes. "Just kiss me already!"

"No pressure, though, right?"

Kelsi had enough of his nonsense at that point, so she grabbed the front of his shirt in her hand and pulled him down toward her, planting her lips on his. If the mountain wouldn't kiss Mohammed…or something like that.

For a moment, Shane was too shocked by her abruptness to respond, but then he decided he liked it too much to care who had initiated the kiss. His arms wrapped around her and he pulled her closer, deepening the kiss.

When she pulled back a minute later, her eyes were glazed. "Now that, my friend, is a kiss."

"Friend?" he asked, one eyebrow raised. "I don't usually kiss friends that way."

"Glad to hear it," she managed to say, though her heart beat out of control. "Maybe we should watch the rest of the movie."

"Why? You didn't like it?" Had she not felt what he had during the kiss? Had she found it lacking somehow?

"I liked it too much. Stop distracting me from my slasher spoof." She turned back to face the television, sitting up straight this time, not putting her head on his shoulder. Never had a kiss made her feel the way that one did. What was it about good ol' Sheriff Shane that made her stomach feel as if butterflies had taken up residence there?

Shane pushed play on the remote and put his arm back around her shoulders, straightening the blanket covering them both. He'd passed the "kiss test" he didn't know he'd be taking...not that he could have studied for it. Was she always going to leave him confused and reeling?

Chapter Three

SHANE WATCHED the clock the following morning, looking forward to the moment when he could see Kelsi for lunch at the café. They'd only shared the one kiss the night before, but it had knocked his socks off. He had a feeling she'd felt the same.

He completed some of the paperwork he'd put off the day before, and when it was finally time to go to lunch, he grabbed his hat and hurried out the door. He was nervous about seeing her, worried she might have decided going out with him had been a mistake. He'd waited for her for so long that he was ready to take their relationship to the next level, but he was sure she wasn't yet. She would need time to get used to the fact that they belonged together.

When he arrived at the café, it was still too early for the lunch rush. He'd deliberately timed it so he could have ten or fifteen minutes before the other customers swooped in for lunch. Sitting in the same booth he had used the day before, and most days for the past four years, he waited until she came out of the kitchen to greet him.

Liz, the only other waitress on duty that day, knew

better than to wait on him, as Kelsi always took care of him herself. She did acknowledge him with a nod, though, as she continued filling the salt and pepper shakers.

Kelsi walked toward him with the usual bounce in her step. "Hey, you!" she said as she slipped into the booth across from him. She was wearing a knee-length black skirt, a white sweater, and the same red cowboy boots she'd worn the night before. He wasn't sure what it was about those red cowboy boots, but every time he caught a glimpse of them on her, he couldn't help but grin.

"Hi!" It didn't feel awkward seeing her at all, as he'd been slightly worried it would. "How's Dani doing with the cooking?"

"She's mad at everyone, and if I don't hire someone within the next week, she's going to glue my hair to my pillow and put shampoo on my toothbrush." Kelsi rolled her eyes. "Always the same threats. I'll find someone as soon as I can, but it probably won't be tomorrow. It's not like we have a huge metropolis to pull from!"

Shane reached out and took her hand in his, not caring if Liz saw them. The waitress was the only other person in the front part of the café with them. "What are you doing on Saturday night?" His thumb brushed along her palm.

"I want to go for a hike Saturday afternoon. Do you want to go? I asked Will, and he said he's sick of hiking with me." Kelsi frowned at him. "You're not sick of hiking with me yet, are you?"

Shane frowned. "We've never hiked together, so I couldn't be sick of hiking with you. Why do you say *yet*?"

Kelsi shrugged. "Everyone always gets sick of hiking with me eventually. I usually have to bribe my siblings to go."

"What do you bribe them with?" he asked, intrigued.

Surely not money, because they were all equally wealthy. It had to be something good though.

"I offer to make Dani's bed for a week. With the guys, I've offered to cook their next Sunday night dinner here at the café. We take turns hosting Sunday dinners, but they all have better things they'd rather do." She hated cooking too, but if it got her a hiking partner on occasion, it was worth it. It really wasn't safe to hike alone in the wilderness, and a good portion of the ranch was just that.

"Your family does Sunday night dinners?" With all the gossip in town about their family, that was one thing he'd never heard.

She nodded. "We always have. We had them with Grandma Kelsey and Granddad Wilfred when I was little, and then as the boys grew up and moved to their own houses across the highway, we kept having them, because it's the one time every week when we all get to sit and talk."

The very idea of a weekly dinner with her boisterous family made him shudder. "So why does everyone get sick of hiking with you?"

"Oh, they think I take too long looking for signs and taking pictures. And something about how they hate my choice of topic." She shrugged, an innocent expression on her face, but he had a feeling whatever she was hiding wasn't so innocent.

Shane tilted his head to one side, studying her. "What aren't you telling me? What's the topic?"

Kelsi leaned forward, obviously ready to speak in confidence. "You can't tell anyone."

He shook his head. "I would never tell anyone what you tell me in confidence."

"Bigfoot lives in the mountains on the other side of the river. I'm looking for signs of Bigfoot."

He blinked a few times. "You're kidding, right?"

She shook her head. "Nope. Dead serious. So, you going Bigfoot hunting with me on Saturday afternoon?"

"As long as you don't mean actual hunting where we'd kill a humanoid creature, sure. I'll help you search for Bigfoot." They wouldn't find anything, he was sure, because if Bigfoot had once lived in the mountains of her ranch, he'd be long gone, finding an area that was less populated. Of course, Bigfoot didn't exist, so he didn't know why he was thinking that anyway.

She bounced a little, squealing. "I'll reserve the four-wheelers, and we'll ride out across the bridge over the river on those, and then cover the lower portion of one of the mountains from there. This is my first time to go out all year!"

He frowned. "Exactly how long have you been searching for Bigfoot?"

"Since I was ten!"

He sighed. "And you haven't found him yet?"

"Not yet, but we will this weekend! I just know it!" Kelsi frowned when she saw her brother, Will, enter the café. "What do you want?"

"Just making sure you're okay." Will slid into the booth beside Kelsi, trapping her between himself and the wall. "I don't trust the sheriff with my baby sister. You know that…"

"Whatever. He's going Bigfoot hunting with me this weekend," she whispered excitedly.

Will laughed. "You've got it bad, don't you?" he asked Shane.

Shane frowned. "She said you go with her sometimes!"

"We only go to make sure she doesn't kill herself by falling in the river or tumbling down a mountain. We don't actually *help* her search for Bigfoot."

Shane's eyes stayed steady on Will's. *Did her brother really think he was that stupid?* "We'll need two of the ATVs." He knew the ranch had several that could be rented by the guests of the ranch.

"Sorry, only one available."

"We'll share," Kelsi announced. "I'll pack a good lunch for us, and we'll explore. It'll be fun!"

"*So* much fun!" Will said with exaggerated enthusiasm.

Shane decided to ignore her brother. "We could watch another movie tonight, or I can take you into town and we can go to the diner?" He knew seeing her every single night wasn't going to be an option, but he wanted it to be.

Kelsi shrugged. "Or I could fix us dinner at your place," she suggested.

Shane thought for a moment about whether he'd left his dirty laundry on the floor. "That would work for me. I'll help you cook if you want?"

"Nah. How 'bout Mexican food? I'm in the mood for some enchiladas."

Will looked at Shane. "She's a good cook, but if you're going for Mexican, you might need to have a fire extinguisher available."

Shane shrugged, determined not to let her brother frighten him. "If she can handle it, I can handle it." He'd practically cut his teeth on spicy foods.

Will got out of the booth, shaking his head. "You're making a mistake, but it's your tongue that will be burned off, not mine." He looked at Shane. "The woman has a cast iron stomach. No one can out-spice her."

Shane watched as Will left, then looked at Kelsi. "I grew up in Southern California. I can handle whatever you can."

Kelsi grinned. "Works for me." She took the key he offered her.

"You're welcome to go over and start cooking whenever you're ready."

"You'll be home shortly after five?" she asked.

He nodded. "Yup."

She scooted out of the booth, slipping his key in the pocket of her apron. "What are you having for lunch?"

"Tuesday Special," he responded, wondering if she'd ever give him a menu again. Not that he cared, because he really didn't need one.

"Medium-rare?"

"Is there any other way to eat a steak?"

"I prefer mine not to be mooing," she said, heading for the kitchen.

She gave Dani the order and watched as her sister dropped fries into the hot oil and slapped a steak on the stove. "I want my boots back. You're going to scuff them."

"If I do, I'll buy you a new pair," Kelsi responded, leaning on the counter, watching her sister cook. "I'm going to cook for Shane tonight."

Dani raised an eyebrow at her. "That's a whole lot of sheriff in a short amount of time."

"*My* life." Kelsi knew her siblings would wonder about her spending so much time with him, because she hadn't spent even one evening a week with Donn for the past six years.

Dani shrugged, turning back to her cooking. "Have you placed an ad for a cook yet?"

"Not yet. I'll do it before I go over to the sheriff's tonight."

"Please do. I don't want to pull double-duty forever."

"I will," Kelsi promised as she wandered off to get Shane his drink.

* * *

Kelsi wasn't sure what to expect when she let herself into Shane's house that afternoon with an armful of groceries.

Kicking the front door closed, she wandered through the living area and into the kitchen, finally setting the bags down. The house wasn't a mansion, by any means, but was certainly larger than her living space at the ranch house, which consisted of her bedroom and the bathroom she shared with her sister.

Each of her brothers had a home across the highway from the main house, but were still on ranch land. She and Dani were the only two still left in their ancestral home, which was probably good. It left more rooms to be rented out to guests during the busy summer season.

Kelsi dug through Shane's cabinets to find what she needed, while noting how organized he was. It was surprising to find a man who was so obviously strong with such a well-organized kitchen. Of course, Shane was always one to keep people guessing. How many sheriffs could double as a short-order cook on the weekends?

Once she had the enchiladas in the oven, she wandered through the house, looking at everything. The way a man kept his home said a lot about him, and she was curious about Shane.

His dirty laundry was in the hamper, a towel thrown haphazardly onto the dresser. Everything else was neat. There was no razor out, but he wore a neatly-trimmed beard so he probably didn't shave every day.

There were three bedrooms. The first was obviously occupied by him, and was decorated in dark blues and browns, colors she thought of as masculine. His bed was left unmade, but she couldn't say anything about that. If she hadn't needed to keep her bed made because she lived in the main house, she wouldn't have.

She stuck her head into the first of the spare rooms and

noted it had a twin-sized bed but was primarily used for an office.

The other room had a bed underneath a pile of random junk. Kelsi smiled. She was sure if she had a house of this size to herself, one of the bedrooms would be a junk room as well. She stuck her head in the other bathroom before wandering back through the dining room to the kitchen. The house wasn't huge by any means, but it was just about right for a small family.

She hurriedly worked on the salad while the enchiladas finished baking, and then she opened a can of refried beans. Normally when Kelsi cooked, she did everything from scratch. She didn't buy anything in a can. She would usually soak the beans and then mash them into refried herself, but she hadn't had a lot of time on such short notice.

She made a box of Spanish rice, cringing as she used it. Not cooking often meant she did it right, and didn't use a lot of processed foods.

Kelsi was just pulling the enchiladas out of the oven when she heard the front door open and close. She smiled at Shane as he walked into the kitchen, still wearing his uniform. She'd never been one of those girls who couldn't resist a man in uniform, but Shane in uniform was a different story. Shane in anything made her heart beat faster.

"Dinner will be ready in about ten minutes. Do you want to go change first? Or let me look at you in your uniform all night?"

He raised an eyebrow. "You like the uniform?" If it would earn him extra points with her, he'd wear it all night.

She shrugged. "On you, I do. I like you in jeans too, though."

"I'm going to go put jeans on then. I get tired of wearing this."

She smiled sweetly as he walked away, her eyes appreciating the view she had of his shoulders and backside. When he turned and caught her looking, she winked at him.

By the time he returned, she had their plates on the table with water poured for each of them. One of the first things she'd noticed about Shane was that he always drank water with his meals, which pleased her. It was her favorite thing to drink as well.

He came into the dining room and smelled the air. "Smells delicious. What kind of enchiladas did you make?"

"Beef with a tomato sauce. If I'd had more time, I'd have done it all from scratch, and knocked your socks off, but there wasn't much time today. Next time."

He walked to her and leaned down, kissing her cheek. It felt strange to be able to be so familiar with her after so much time having to keep his distance, but he was glad he could now. "Thanks for cooking for me, even if it wasn't from scratch."

"Next time!"

He shook his head. "Next time I'll cook for you!"

Kelsi smiled at that. "You can cook for me as often as you want. I'd rather sit back and watch anyway."

He sat down at the head of the table, and she took the spot to one side of him. "I'm impressed. I had it in my head you couldn't cook at all, even warming stuff up, because you never do at the café."

"I'm needed up front at the café. When we do need extra people, we always need a cook. We don't have as much turnover with the wait staff as we do the cooks." Besides, her sister had never been trustworthy when it came to dealing with guests or customers. She was too volatile.

"Is Dani still annoyed she's being forced to cook?"

"Yup. And today she was annoyed because I was wearing her boots. She just has to be grumpy about something." She took a bite of her enchilada, feeling the heat as the pepper burned her tongue. She smiled. "That's perfect."

Shane took a bite as well, remembering her brother's warning. He wasn't going to wimp out, so he took a big bite, knowing he could handle it. He'd grown up eating Mexican food after all.

Kelsi watched as he took a bite, chewed for a moment, and began fanning his mouth. He quickly grabbed his water, and downed it before going for more.

As he was gulping a second glass of water at the kitchen sink, she said, "Get yourself some more enchiladas from the other end of the pan. I made those with less peppers. I'll take yours." She helped herself to the enchiladas on his plate, continuing to eat calmly as if they weren't spicy at all.

"How do you eat that?" he asked, gasping and shaking his head at her. He was sure he would have a blister on his tongue if he checked in a mirror.

She shrugged. "It's how I like it. I've learned to make a few for me, and milder ones for everyone else, though."

He carefully took a tiny bite of the new enchilada, obviously concerned it would still be too spicy. It *was* still hot, but it didn't threaten to burn through his tongue, and leave a hole in the roof of his mouth, so he took a bigger bite.

"These are really good if you don't mind third degree burns on your tongue."

After the meal, she put the dishes into the sink, saving

the food that was left. She carefully put the spicy enchiladas into a bowl to take home with her, and the rest went into the refrigerator for him.

"If I cook, I don't do dishes," she told him, walking out of the kitchen with the dishes all piled in the sink.

He shrugged. "Sounds fair. I can do them after you leave."

"You kicking me out?"

"Not at all. I thought maybe you'd want to stay for a little while. We could watch television."

She made a face. "It's Tuesday. Do you mind if we watch *Lazy Love*? I don't usually watch sappy TV shows, but there's just something about that one. I think Jesse Savoy is pretty darn sexy, even though he's not a real cowboy." She'd been watching the show since the first episode, and she just couldn't look away. It was her guilty pleasure, and she wasn't going to hide it from him.

Shane laughed, shaking his head. "I have only seen a few episodes of the show."

"Oh, really? I love it. The two main actors got married in real life last month, and there was a lot of talk about it in the tabloids because she was dating someone else. She married her co-star as soon as she split with the other guy. I hear they're really happy, though."

He led her into the living room, sitting in the middle of the couch so she could sit on either side of him, but she'd be snuggled against him either way. "What channel?"

After she told him, he used the remote to turn it on. "Do you watch this at home?"

She nodded. "Every single week."

As they waited for the show to start, she told him a little about the series, wanting him to understand what he was about to watch.

Her phone rang while she was in mid-explanation. She

fished it out of her purse, frowning down at it. "It's my mom. Gotta take it." She swiped her finger across the screen. "Hey, Mom."

"Kelsi, why didn't you call and tell me when you broke up with Donn?"

"Why would I give you any details about my life when I know your spies are going to tell you everything within a couple of hours anyway?" Kelsi asked, winking at Shane who was watching her intently.

"Because it's not polite to let your mother hear everything about your life from other people! You should call and tell me these things!"

"Sorry, Mom. Donn moved to California to make cotton candy for Disneyland. I'm dating Sheriff Shane now." Kelsi knew her mother already had more information than she would have given her. It was crazy the things she heard from halfway across the country.

"So I heard. Well, you won't have to date him for long."

Kelsi blinked. "I *like* dating him, Mom."

"Well, forget him for a minute. When I got the call yesterday that Kathy had quit, I was so sad for you. I know how much Dani dislikes working in the café, but of course, you had to go to your sister for help. Well, we found this nice little diner in a tiny town in Louisiana, and the food was wonderful. You know me, when the food is good, I always ask to meet the chef, and the man who came out to talk to us looked so familiar."

Kelsi sighed, really not wanting to know where the story was going. Shane was watching her intently, like he knew something was happening that he wouldn't like. "And? Did you know him?"

"Not really him, but I knew his father before he moved away. Do you remember cute little Bobby Blakely?"

"Bobby Blakely wasn't cute, Mom! He chased me around at recess with whatever reptiles he could find. Dani too. He couldn't tell us apart, so he decided to be in love with both of us. He was just awful! I felt like I'd won the lottery when they moved away after third grade!" Kelsi rolled her eyes at Shane, her hand reaching out to grip his.

"He was a good boy. You and your sister were adorable and the only identical twins in school. Of course, he liked you. Anyway, that man was cute little Bobby Blakely all grown up!"

Kelsi groaned. "Please tell me you didn't offer him a job! I don't want to have to work with Bobby Blakely!" She couldn't think of anyone she less wanted to work with every day.

"Of course I offered him a job. And do you know what, Kelsi Jo? I think he's the perfect man for you. You should marry him."

Kelsi counted to ten before she responded to her mother. "I can't marry him, Mom. I'm dating a man who carries a gun. You don't want Bobby to *die* to you?"

"Sheriff Clapper isn't going to kill Bobby for marrying you. He'll understand that the better man won the girl. It's that simple!"

"I don't think Shane is going to consider Bobby the better man."

"He had to give two weeks' notice, but he's going to leave for Idaho a week from Monday. I'm sure you'll be sick of the sheriff by then."

The call ended abruptly, and Kelsi looked at it for a minute, wanting to throw it across the room. "Bobby Blakely has been hired to cook for the café, and it doesn't matter that I have never liked Bobby Blakely. He was the most annoying boy in the whole elementary school, but Mom has decided he's the perfect husband for me. She probably already gave him my ring size so he can have one in his pocket when he arrives." She leaned back against the couch and groaned. "I'm *not* going to marry Bobby Blakely!"

"Did you just tell your mother I would shoot him if he married you?" Shane asked, trying to understand all of what he'd heard.

"Well, I didn't exactly tell her you'd shoot him, but I may have implied it wouldn't be good for his health if he married me. You do carry a gun for work after all."

Shake shook his head at her, trying not to laugh. "Your mother has always been a force to be reckoned with."

"Do you know they're letting us run the ranch for now, but they are reserving the right to not leave the ranch to us if they don't feel like it? There's going to be some kind of big test, and they won't even tell us what the big test *is*!"

He pulled her against him, his arm going around her shoulders. "Let's watch your show. It'll make you feel better."

"I hope Bob isn't annoying on this episode." Kelsi couldn't deal with another annoying Bob at the moment, even if this one was on TV.

"Bob?"

"He's the ranch foreman. He thinks he's supposed to marry Jo, because that's what Jo's dad wanted before he died. What is it about parents wanting their kids to marry Bobs? I refuse! I will not be a Bob-lover, and no one can make me!"

"No one is going to turn you into a Bob-lover on my watch! A Shane-lover is more what we're looking for in this town!"

"I'm not promising to be a Shane-lover either. Right now, I'm promising to be a spicy food-lover and a Bigfoot-lover. Nothing else!"

"Fine. I'm going to wear you down, though." As they watched the opening for *Lazy Love*, he said softly, "And if it gets too intense with Bob the cook, just remember, there's a Shane that's always willing to get you away from that nonsense?"

Kelsi looked at him, seeing that he was watching her and not the opening credits. "Oh yeah? How?"

"I'll marry you myself."

Kelsi jerked her eyes back to the television, not sure how to respond to that. It had taken almost two years of dating Donn before she'd realized she had no desire to ever marry him. The first time he'd asked her out, she'd been sure he was the man of her dreams, but he wasn't. He was nothing of the sort.

How could she know that her feelings for Shane wouldn't go the same route, and soon she'd think of him the same way she'd thought of Donn? Donn had ended up being no more than a fashion accessory at the end of their relationship. If she'd married him, she'd have tied herself forever to a man who bored her to tears.

Shane couldn't help wondering exactly what was rushing through Kelsi's mind. It was obvious her thoughts were on something other than the show they were watching. He wished he could get inside her head so he could know, but he didn't ask. He knew she probably wouldn't have answered him anyway.

Chapter Four

SHANE SENSED something had gone horribly wrong after the phone call with Kelsi's mother on Tuesday, but he wasn't sure what it was. He saw her every day for lunch, but she claimed to be too tired to see him in the evenings. He knew she wasn't used to working all day and spending the evening out, so he believed her, but still worried something wasn't quite right.

He couldn't put his finger on it, but she was treating him a little differently as well. She seemed distant and wasn't trying to get as close as she did the first couple of nights. When he got to the café early on Saturday morning to work, they were the first people there. "Are we still going hiking this afternoon?"

She nodded. "I packed two backpacks for us, and there's a four-wheeler parked behind the café. I'm ready to leave as soon as we finish up here this afternoon." She moved toward the counter where she was filling up the boxes of sugar they put on the tables.

"Are you upset with me about something?" he asked, watching her reaction carefully.

"Upset with you?" Her brows drew together in a frown. "Why would I be upset with you?" He hadn't done anything to upset her.

Shane shrugged. "You seem to be keeping me at a distance, and you weren't at first."

Kelsi sighed. "It was something my mom said to me. She told me I'd be sick of you within a few weeks and ready to move on to Bobby. I don't think I will, but she's right that I got sick of Donn rather quickly." She shrugged. "I don't want to mess up our relationship, but I'm worried." She'd never known a man to hold her interest for long.

"And you think the closer we get, the quicker you'll get sick of me and be ready to move on?"

"I hope not! But it is kind of my history."

Shane took her hand and walked to a booth with her. They had a half hour before opening, so they could take ten minutes to talk. When he slid into the same side with her, she gave him a startled look. He'd never done that before.

"What attracted you to Donn?" he asked.

"I'm really not sure. My friends all talked about how cute he was, and I guess I thought he was cute too. He was the most popular boy in school, and having him ask me out was kind of flattering." She shrugged. She'd never really considered why she'd gone out with Donn, but she didn't remember ever being attracted to him. Not the way she was to Shane.

"Did his kisses ever make your toes curl?"

Kelsi laughed softly. "I don't recall ever having that particular reaction to his kisses." Only one man's kisses had ever affected her so strongly, and he was sitting beside her. Of course, maybe she just hadn't kissed enough men. She'd dated a couple of guys in high

50

school, and then she'd had a long relationship with Donn.

"And *my* kisses? What do my kisses make you feel?"

She blushed. "I don't know…I…"

"How 'bout I remind you?" he asked. They hadn't kissed since their date on Monday night, because she'd seemed so awkward around him all of a sudden. There was a special vibrancy to Kelsi that had been missing, and he needed it to come back to her. Cupping her face in both hands, he leaned down, gently brushing his lips across hers.

Kelsi sighed softly, her arms wrapping around his neck as she leaned in closer for a deeper kiss. "*You* make my toes curl," she finally whispered.

"Then don't you think it's worth it to see where our relationship goes? It sounds to me like we already have more going for us than you and Donn The Dipstick ever had."

"How many derogatory D-words are people going to come up with for Donn?"

"No idea. They keep coming to me like magic sprinkles from the sky!" He stroked one thumb across her lips. "Do you feel better?"

She nodded. "I think so. I just worry, and I don't ever want to disappoint you." He was too special for her to mess with. Besides, who needed the law in town angry with them?

He pressed one more kiss to her lips. "You never could. Just keep being you, Kelsi."

He slid out of the booth and walked into the kitchen to heat up the grill and get everything organized for the morning.

Kelsi watched him go, thinking about what a good man he was. He put up with so much from everyone in town —including her.

Saturdays were the biggest days in the café, and she rushed in and out of the kitchen all morning, passing Liz and Joni repeatedly. When the rush was finally over, and the café was closed, Shane made them all lunch.

Kelsi and Shane sat together in one booth, and Liz and Joni sat in the other. The two girls had a tight-knit relationship that Kelsi always wished she had with other girls. She was close to her sister and to their cousin, Jess, who had been raised with them, but she didn't have a lot of other female friends. Spending all her time working after school in high school and college did that to a woman. Whenever she saw Liz and Joni together, she felt like she was missing out on something.

Shane watched as she picked at the chicken casserole he'd made. "Is something wrong with the food?"

"Not spicy enough. Getting seasoning." She jumped up and ran to the kitchen, coming back with some Cajun seasoning that she applied liberally to her meal.

"That spicy enough now?" he asked, frowning at all the extra seasoning. No one had ever said he didn't use enough seasoning before.

She took a bite of the casserole. "I think so. Want to try?"

"I guess." He took a bite of her food and almost choked, reaching for his water glass to ease the burning in his mouth. "I don't know that we're ever going to be able to cook for each other."

"Don't worry. I carry a small can of this in my purse. I'll be fine." She tended to add it to just about everything, something Grandma Kelsey had taught her as well. She missed her grandmother every day.

He applied himself to his bacon cheeseburger. "I don't know where your taste buds got broken, but it's a sad thing.

Do you always have to have that much spice to enjoy food?"

"Mostly. I mean, I eat food with less spice, but not happily." She looked up as the door to the café opened and her brother Wyatt walked in. "Hey, Wyatt."

"Do you have any carrots leftover?" her brother asked. Wyatt was a man of few words, so Kelsi was always pleased when he sought her out for any reason.

"I think so." She looked at Shane. "Carrots?" He'd know better than she would.

Shane nodded. "In the bottom vegetable drawer on the left."

"Do you need me to get them for you?" Kelsi offered, knowing her brother didn't often go into the café's kitchen.

Wyatt shook his head. "I got it." His eyes landed on Shane. "Heard you two were dating." That's all he said before he wandered off, not mentioning how he felt about them dating at all. It was almost refreshing to not have someone share their opinion with them.

Shane watched him go. "I don't think he's ever said that much to me all at once before."

"He must need the carrots for treats for the horses. I know a couple of them prefer carrots to anything else." Wyatt was all about his equine friends, often leading guests of the ranch on overnight trail rides.

Her brother came back from the kitchen, holding up a bag of carrots before leaving. Kelsi watched him go, wondering what went on in his head. Even as kids, he was the brother least likely to tease her or talk to her about anything.

Kelsi finished her casserole and pushed it away. "I'm stuffed."

"Me too. Let's get the dishes in the dishwasher and head out." He looked at the two waitresses at the other table, who appeared to be finished, but engrossed in conversation. "You ladies done eating?"

Liz nodded. "Yeah, we'll get out of here." She smiled at Joni, heading toward the door. "I have so much I want to get done today."

Joni shrugged. "You always do."

Kelsi slid out of the booth and gathered some of the dishes, Shane right behind her with the rest of them.

Ten minutes later, she locked up the café, grabbed the backpacks out from under the counter, went out to the four-wheeler, and put on a pink helmet. Shane was pleased to see there was a black helmet for him, but he frowned when she got on the front of the four-wheeler.

"I'm driving," he said quietly.

She shook her head. "Nope. I know where I want to go, and I love driving these things. Hang on, Sheriff. You're in for a ride." She wasn't going to back down and let him drive. It was *her* quest for Bigfoot, and she was going to drive her favorite of the ranch's toys. Well, the four-wheelers and the snowmobiles were both her favorites. She could happily spend all her time outdoors.

She started the four-wheeler, and the look she gave him made it clear that she was going with or without him, so if he wanted to accompany her, he'd better climb on.

Shane sighed but climbed on, his arms going around her waist. As soon as he was seated, she took off, going along the side of the driveway that led through the property to the main ranch house. They drove past the spa, the main house, and the parking lot before crossing the bridge that would take them to the other side of the river and the mountains.

She drove along the river for a bit before stopping at a wide spot along the bank. "This is where we need to start looking again," she told him. "I keep finding berry bushes that the Bigfoot have been eating along here."

He sighed. "How do you know it's Bigfoot and not deer?"

"I just know." She climbed off the four-wheeler, pocketing the key. She was wearing jeans and a flannel shirt, along with a light spring jacket. "Come on! I bet we see one today! I brought my camera!" She was excited to share this part of her life with him—a part no one else had ever willingly wanted to share.

"Of course, you did!" he said. He'd said he'd hunt for Bigfoot with her, and whether it had been a sincere offer on his part or not, he was going to keep up his end of the bargain. "What made you decide Bigfoot lived in the mountains here?"

She shrugged. "I guess it's something I've always known. Every time I saw one of those 'Search for Bigfoot' shows, I knew this is where they'd be found." She gave him a radiant smile. "Thanks for believing in me."

He reached over to grasp her hand. "Let's find Bigfoot." He didn't believe in her as much as he believed she shouldn't be in the wilderness by herself, but he wasn't about to tell her that. No, he would happily join her quest, because it meant time together to get to know one another.

As they traipsed through the brush, she showed him little things that she was sure meant Bigfoot was close. A half-eaten berry bush, a trail, and even a large footprint. The footprint astounded him, because the snow had only been melted for a few days. Why would there already be a bare footprint on the still rather cold ground? It really *could* be a Bigfoot, but she didn't seem overly excited by it.

When she didn't take a picture of the footprint, instead moving on, he questioned her. "No picture of the footprint?" She'd taken snaps of the berries and the trail, which he was sure had been made by rabbits.

She shook her head. "My brothers, Will and Wesley, made a huge mold when we were teenagers. When they know I'm going to come out here searching, one of them will sneak out first and use the mold to make it look like the creatures are close. They've been doing it for years. When they're with me, I act all excited, so they'll keep wasting their time, but I'm on to them."

Shane shook his head. "How can you keep letting them think they're getting you that way? Doesn't that make you crazy?"

"Because I know I'm getting them too. It keeps me going on sleepless nights." Kelsi led the way through the underbrush up the side of the mountain. He knew this wasn't one of the mountains they used for skiing or it wouldn't be quite so overgrown. He knew the Westons had two mountains that they had ski hills set up on though.

When he noticed she was out of breath, he said he needed a break, and they sat down on a couple of rocks to drink the water she'd packed into their backpacks. As he dug through the things she'd brought, he realized she really was an Idaho girl, born and bred. She had everything they could possibly need for any eventuality from frostbite to sunburn. No one ever knew what the weather was going to be, so preparing for everything was always the best course of action.

"How much higher will we go?" he asked, barely able to see the four-wheeler off in the distance.

She shrugged. "What time is it?"

"It's after five. If we don't head back, we're going to get caught out after dark." He was disappointed to have to end their time together, but he really didn't want to get caught out after dark. It wasn't safe. Apparently, there were Bigfoot around.

She sighed. "I hate going back without finding Bigfoot."

"We'll try again."

"You mean it?" she asked, having expected him to come with her once and be done. Donn had never been willing to come with her, and her siblings made fun of her the whole time.

"Absolutely. Whether we find Bigfoot or not, I enjoy spending time with you. I think you're pretty special, you know."

Kelsi smiled, moving over to join him on his rock. "I think you're special too. Thank you so much for not laughing and for coming up here with me. I enjoy it out here so much, Bigfoot notwithstanding."

"Do you use Bigfoot as an excuse to get out and see nature?" he asked, suddenly feeling like he understood what she was up to.

She shook her head adamantly. "No, but I love being out here. Bigfoot is my primary concern though. I'm going to find him, and when I do, my brothers will have to eat a whole lot of crow...why, I'll even bake it into a pie for them."

"A pie with jalapenos?"

"What else would you put in crow pie?" she asked, resting her head on his shoulder for just a moment. "We need to come on a day when we're both off the entire day, so we'll have more time to find one."

"Whenever you want," he answered. Truthfully, he enjoyed hiking as much as she did. If she wanted to call it Bigfoot hunting, he wouldn't complain too much.

Together they made their way down the mountain and

back to the four-wheeler. "Can I drive you into town for dinner tonight?"

She nodded slowly, getting on the front of the four-wheeler. "As long as we don't go anywhere fancy. I don't feel like changing."

"I hope you don't ever change," he said into her ear after putting his helmet on. He looked down at the river which was raging below them. "Look at how full the river is."

She nodded. "Lots of snowfall this year. So as the snow is melting, the mountain streams are filling and they're all dumping into the river. The lake is crazy high, right about now." The lake she mentioned was on her family's property as well. The ranch got its name from the river emptying into the lake, making it the end of the river.

"Do you ever go out on the river?" he asked.

She nodded. "And on the lake. It's Will's favorite thing, of course, and he's the brother I'm closest to, so we do stuff like that together sometimes."

"I'd love to go with you."

She smiled over her shoulder at him as she started the four-wheeler, taking the same route back as she'd taken to get there, because there was only one bridge over the river. You could go all the way south of the lake, but that seemed to take too long in Kelsi's estimation.

Once they'd reached the shed where the four-wheelers were kept, she climbed off and tucked her helmet under her arm. "This one is mine, but I borrowed yours."

"Leave it on the four-wheeler?" he asked.

She nodded. "Someone will be by to put it up in a little while." They were a good ten-minute walk from the house and five minutes from the café. "Why don't we go get my truck from the ranch house, and I'll drive us this evening?"

"That works." He held her hand as they made the walk

back to the ranch house. "I don't think I ever realized just how much property your family owns. I mean, I've seen it on a map, but being out there and driving around is different."

"Yeah. It's a massive property." And she loved every little piece of it. It was home in a way nothing else ever could be.

Once they reached the ranch house, he stopped. "Do you want to leave right away? Or go in for a bit?"

She shrugged. "Let's just go. Less chance of running into any of my family members that way."

"I heard that!" Kelsi turned, immediately recognizing Will's voice. "Must you always be difficult?"

"See any signs of Bigfoot?" Will asked.

"We did! There were several perfect impressions of his foot! It was amazing!" Kelsi's voice was filled with excitement.

"Really?" Will asked, wide-eyed. "How do you know it was him?"

"Because even *your* feet aren't *that* big!" Kelsi told him. "And your feet need to be chopped off at the toes to be considered normal-sized!"

Will shook his head. "Not all of us can be teeny-tiny little creatures who would do well working to build toys for Santa."

Kelsi wrinkled her nose. "I'm not an elf, I'm just the perfect size. Ask Shane."

"Everything about her is perfect from what I can see," Shane answered honestly. "I wouldn't change a single thing about her."

"There are days when you make me want to vomit, Sheriff. This is one of them." Will winked at his sister and walked away.

Kelsi unlocked the door to her truck and climbed up

via the little step Will had installed when she bought it, laughing at her the whole while. "Where are we going?" she asked, hoping Shane wanted to go further than Riston. She would only run into people she knew there, and she was tired of her every move being reported back to her mother.

"Let's go to Post Falls. I want something different."

Kelsi grinned, feeling like he could read her mind at times. She pulled out of the parking lot and onto the drive that led to the highway. "I love driving!"

"I know. I remember having to pull you over a couple of times when you were still a teenager because of your lead foot."

"You're not supposed to remember that. You're supposed to see me and only think of how wonderful I am…not about the way I drove when I was a teenager." She pulled out onto the highway, heading toward Post Falls. "Where do you want to eat?"

"I dunno. They have that steak place there. That sound good?"

"Sure, why not?" They'd been driving for about ten minutes when her phone rang, and she frowned. "Answer that and put it on speaker for me, please." She pulled it from her pocket and gave it to him.

"It's your mom."

"Oh, yay. I haven't heard from her about how I need to marry Bobby yet today."

He frowned, hating the idea of her being pressured to marry someone else. He wanted her to be pressured to marry him. Swiping his finger across the screen, he tapped the speaker phone button.

"Hello?" Kelsi said.

"Hi. I heard you spent all day with the sheriff again. When are you going to get over your need to find Bigfoot?"

"Hi, Mom, I love you too! You're on speaker phone, and I'm still with Shane."

"Hi, Sheriff. I hope you know that you're not the right man for my daughter. You'll have to stop dating her in about ten days when Bobby gets back to Idaho."

"I'm not going to date Bobby, Mom."

"Are you still holding a grudge against him for the reptile-thing?" her mother asked. "It's about time you forgot about that."

"It's not the reptile-thing. It's the I-don't-know-him-thing. And I kind of have a 'thing' for the sheriff." She stopped at a four-way stop, and reached over to squeeze his hand before driving again.

"You just started dating the sheriff. I'm sure you're not that attached yet."

"What if I'm that attached to her, Mrs. Weston? What about my heart breaking into a million tiny little pieces because Bobby is coming back to town?" Shane couldn't stay silent for another minute. If Kelsi was receiving similar calls every day, no wonder she was confused.

"You'll get over her. She's practically engaged to Bobby."

"Mom, I'm not 'practically engaged to Bobby.' I have feelings for *Shane*." What those feelings were was something she had yet to explore, but there was something there.

"Feelings and being in love are two different things. Can either of you honestly say you love the other?"

Kelsi felt put on the spot, and she frowned. "I can't tell you I love him before I tell *him*," she finally said, needing an escape from the question.

"I can say it honestly. I love Kelsi. I've had my eye on her for years and I'm glad she and Donn The Disgusting finally broke up."

Kelsi felt her lips quirk at the new name for Donn. "See, Mom? You have to quit pushing Bobby at me."

"Fine. I won't say anything else about it right now."

Kelsi sighed, knowing she'd hear a lot more about it later. "Okay, Mom."

"Have a good time with the sheriff. You two should do something fun so you can have some memories together before you split up."

"Mom, you said you'd stop!"

When there was no response, Shane looked at her phone. "She ended the call."

"Of course she did. She makes me crazy sometimes!" Kelsi shook her head. "Don't listen to her. I can date whoever I want, when I want."

Shane frowned. "She's not going to let up, is she?"

"Not unless I break up with you and date Bobby, but that's not happening." *Break up?* Had they ever decided they were exclusive? The idea of him dating someone else wasn't a pleasant one.

"So let's get married instead. I think that's where we're headed. Why waste time? Especially if your mom is going to be like that. I think it makes sense for us to just get it over with."

"Did you just ask me to marry you with the words 'get it over with' involved? Because that's not quite as romantic as I would like a proposal to be."

He groaned. "I guess I did. What a jerk I am. I'll do better next time."

"Next time?" She pulled into the parking lot of the restaurant he'd suggested and shut off the truck. "There's going to be a next time?"

"I'm going to keep asking over and over until you agree to marry me. I haven't made that clear yet?"

She sighed. "You're going to make this difficult, aren't you?"

He shrugged. "Not if you say yes. Just think, your mom would never suggest you divorce me to marry Bobby. She'd be off your back, and he'd never be a problem again." His voice was intense. He wasn't offering to keep her from being with Bobby. He really wanted to marry her.

"I can't marry you to avoid Bobby Blakely!"

"You could. You just won't." Shane shook his head. He'd find another way. He knew he could. He had to.

Chapter Five

KELSI FROWNED as she watched Shane study his menu. He ignored her until he'd decided what he wanted to eat, and then he put the menu down on the table between them. "Yes?" She didn't usually openly stare the way she was.

"Why do you think you want to marry me?"

"I *know* I want to marry you."

Kelsi sighed. "But *why*?"

"I didn't really know the difference between you and your sister until about four years ago. I knew one of you had shorter, darker hair, and that was about it. You were just 'the Weston girls' in my head. I went to the café for lunch just about every day, but I didn't know which of you was serving me. I honestly didn't care much." He shrugged. "So one day when I got there, there was a waitress in tears. The place was busy, hopping with people, and someone had said something rude to her."

"People tend to be rude to waitresses. They think that we're too stupid to do anything but wait tables. I get a little more respect, because I'm the manager of the café, but it can be really bad." She hated that people didn't seem to understand that all jobs were needed in the world. If there was no one to scrub toilets, the world would fall apart faster than if there was no one to discover a new medical breakthrough.

"You had heard the whole thing, and you marched straight over to the table, put your arm around the waitress's shoulders, and told him he could treat people with respect or he could get out. You went on to tell him that his waitress was special. She was working her way through school with no help from her parents. She was one of the most intelligent people you'd ever met." He shook his head. "Most people I know would have just told her to shake it off and brushed it under the rug for fear of losing a customer. Not you. I was really impressed with that, and I asked one of the other diners which twin you were."

"And you've known who I am every day since then? Interesting. Doesn't tell me why you think you want to marry me, though." Kelsi couldn't figure him out. He was a good-looking sheriff in a tiny little town. She saw the way the groups of women who came in looked at him. He never paid a bit of attention to anyone, other than in a professional way of course. Why her?

"Because you're special. I don't think you know how special." He shook his head. "I can't explain it, but you're not only beautiful, and smart, but you care about people. More than you care about money. That's important to me."

She shrugged. She'd never needed to care about money too much, because her family had always had it. It was Wade's job to make sure the ranch was making money overall, and the café was such a small piece of it. "I guess that makes sense. And you still think I'm smart? Even though you know I go Bigfoot hunting every chance I get?"

He grinned. "I think Bigfoot hunting makes you even more special. You believe in something almost magical, and you refuse to let others convince you it can't be. You take your brother's jokes in stride." He joined hands with her in the middle of the table. "You even kept dating Donn The Dimwit."

"Why is dating Donn points in my favor?" she asked, truly curious and a bit impressed that he kept finding D-word insults for her ex. She wondered if he was poring over the dictionary for new ones every night, or if they just came to him like magic words, raining down from the heavens?

"Because even though you knew you weren't in love with him, you never gave up. If you were married, you'd never ever give up on the relationship. You'd just keep trying. Don't you think that's a good quality in a spouse?"

Kelsi tilted her head to one side, considering. "Yeah, it probably is." She looked down at their joined hands on top of the table. "I can't marry someone I've been dating less than a week." As much as she wanted to please him, it just didn't make sense. Sure, she'd known him for years, but she'd only kissed him for the first time a few days before. It had been an incredible kiss, but she still wasn't convinced.

"Why not? Your mom wants you to marry someone you haven't seen in over ten years. Marry me instead. I promise, I will make you happy!" He felt like time was running out for him with Bobby on the way. Maybe he was being over-dramatic, but her mother was a force to be reckoned with, and he'd rather make her wish impossible before she ever got home to ruin it all.

"You can't guarantee happiness." Kelsi shook her head. "I've watched my parents and grandparents over the years. When Grandma Kelsey died, Granddad Wilfred only lasted a month without her. It was like he no longer cared to live for another minute after she was gone from his life. He became old overnight. That's what I want in a marriage. I want a man who will still be bringing me flowers after fifty years because he knows they make me smile." *And who will still put his hand on the side of my face like he treasures me whenever he kisses me. I want him to not be able to survive without me.*

"I would do that, you know."

She sighed. "Maybe you would, but how can I know that? How can I know exactly what you're like when we've only dated for five days?"

"Think about it. What did you do the last time I didn't come to the café for lunch?"

"I called the sheriff's office to make sure you were still alive. I was sure you'd been in some kind of shoot-out and had died or something!" It had been a scary day when his favorite booth had remained empty. Even the guests told each other to keep that booth open for the sheriff.

"So you called the sheriff's office, and when you heard I was out sick with the flu, you had a delivery of chicken soup sent to my house every single day until I came into the café again. You didn't even know where I lived, and you made that happen for me!"

"Everyone else knew where you lived. What does my doing that say about *you*, though? How does that tell me you'll bring me flowers?"

"Kelsi, I'm there in the café every single day to see you. I could make my own lunch. I could even take leftovers of what I cooked the night before like all my men do. Instead, I'm at the café every day so I can watch you. So I can talk to you. Do you know the other waitresses have been ignoring me for years? I walk in and they don't bother to even greet me. They all know you're supposed to do that."

"But—I never told them to do that!" She was baffled and already planning to have a talk with her staff. They shouldn't be ignoring any of the customers who came in there to eat. Ever.

"Of course, you didn't. They told each other. They saw the way I watched you, and they wanted to see you with a man who was worthy of you, and not that idiot who just left the most amazing woman in the world behind so he could go and make cotton candy for people walking around with mouse ears on their heads!"

"Hey! I happen to like wearing mouse ears on my head!" Was he insulting Disney? Because if he was, they'd have to have a talk.

"Then we'll wear bride and groom mouse ears for our wedding. I don't care!" Shane took a deep breath, wishing he could explain how he was feeling better. "I will be true to you every day of our lives. I want to marry you and have children with you and grow old with you."

Kelsi bit her lip. "I don't know what I feel. And I'm a wreck in relationships. Why would you marry me knowing I might get bored of you in a week?" She didn't think she could ever get bored of a man like him, but if she did, it would ruin both of their lives if they were already married.

"Because I won't let you get bored of me. It doesn't matter if you love me now. I know you'll love me eventually, because I won't let you do anything else."

"Confident in yourself, aren't you?"

"Confident in the fact that we're meant to be together. I want to be married to you before Bobby gets here. You don't need to have that kind of pressure from your mother. You need to be *my* wife instead."

She blinked. "So you not only want to get married, you want to get married before next week?"

"Saturday would be good." He leaned forward, his mouth close to her ear. "I'll even order the mouse ears for the wedding tomorrow."

She smiled at that. "What if I don't want mouse ears? What if I want you to dress up as the Beast, while I dress up as Belle? What if I don't want just any other Disney wedding, and instead I want a *Beauty and the Beast* wedding? She *is* my favorite princess, you know!"

He frowned but nodded. "Then I'll dress up as the Beast. I don't care what either of us wear. I want to marry you."

"Let me think about it. Maybe Mom will back off, and then we can take the time to get to know each other like normal people, instead of acting like we're in a bad romance novel!"

"Okay. You think. Let me know when you've thought long enough."

"I will!"

The waitress came by to take their orders, and Kelsi watched Shane's face. She'd always loved how open and attentive he'd been when she'd taken his orders. It was always obvious she was more than just someone bringing a meal to him. He saw her as a person.

The look was there with this waitress, but it wasn't the same. He wasn't as friendly or open with her. He was still attentive, seeing the waitress as a real human being, but he wasn't as—caring, maybe? She didn't have the right word for what was missing, but she wished she did.

After the waitress walked off, she toyed with Shane's hand still holding hers. "Tell me something. You were always the most attentive customer in the café. You asked me how my day was. If I sat down in the booth across from you, it was not unusual. You invited me to do it. I saw a bit of that on your face with the waitress just now, but not as much as you've ever showed me."

He nodded. "Yeah, that's because she's a person, and I will treat everyone equally, always. What she's not, is you. I knew four years ago that I wanted to marry you. The whole town knew I wanted to marry you. That's what you were seeing."

She frowned, looking down at their joined hands. "And you don't hate me for not realizing?"

"Why would I hate you for that? You were too engrossed in your relationship with Donald Duck to notice me."

"Donald Duck? Did you run out of Donn The D-word names?" she asked, giggling despite herself.

He shrugged. "I can't use all of the good names for him so quick. I'll run out, and where will that leave me?"

As they ate, he noticed she pulled out a small can of Cajun seasoning to sprinkle on her food. "You really do carry a can of that stuff!"

"I told you I did," she said, taking a bite of the potato she'd just heavily sprinkled the seasoning on. "Did you think I was lying?"

"I guess not…I was just surprised. I thought you were joking."

"I never joke about spicy foods. *Never*. You need to learn that now if our relationship is going to go anywhere, Sheriff."

"I'll never question your loyalty to spice again."

"See that you don't!"

Before dinner was over, she'd ignored phone calls from two of her brothers and her cousin, Jess. As soon as they stepped outside, she pulled her phone from her pocket, chilly from the evening air. "I have to figure out why everyone is calling me," she told Shane.

She called Will back, knowing her brother wouldn't have called her while she was on a date unless he considered it important. The others *probably* knew she was out with Shane, but Will definitely did. "What's going on? Someone sick?"

"I called to warn you. Mom is determined you're going to marry little Bobby Blakely. She called me to make sure that I encourage you to date Bobby and not the sheriff. She thinks the sheriff is too old for you and has bad breath."

"Bad breath? Really? I've kissed the man. Trust me, he doesn't have bad breath!" She saw Shane look at her quizzically out of the corner of her eye. "Why is she so determined I marry Bobby?"

"She wants him to start a boxed lunch service. You know, so hikers can pick up picnic lunches before they go out. Or whoever. She thinks it's a service the café should be offering, and she thinks Bobby can do it."

"And Bobby will only do this if we're married?" She didn't understand the logic, but she knew it was her mother's lack of logic, rather than her brother's lack of ability to explain what was happening.

"I have no idea. I've never understood how that woman's mind works. I just wanted to warn you that she was calling all of us. She's—more determined than I've ever seen."

Kelsi sighed, rubbing the back of her neck and the tension there. "I never even liked Bobby Blakely. Remember when I kept coming home crying in elementary school because a mean boy was chasing me around at recess with a snake? And then putting notes in my locker with hearts on them?"

"Yeah."

"That was *Bobby*. He was showing his love by using reptiles!"

Will snorted out a laugh. "He's got a way with women apparently."

"I don't even want to have to work with him, much less marry the idiot! Mom says I need to get over the reptile-thing."

"Well, you probably do need to forgive him for the reptile-thing, but *marry* him? I think you and the sheriff are better-suited."

Kelsi blinked a couple of times in surprise. "You *do*? Why?"

"Because everyone knows how long he's waited to date you, and he's so kind to you. He's what you deserve, Kelsi. Give the man a chance."

She didn't look at Shane as she asked, "But what if I get bored again?"

"Are you really worried about that?" Will asked. "Look, you dated all the popular boys in high school. The ones who were jerks with a capital J. The ones I would have told you to steer clear of if I'd thought you would listen to me. Shane isn't like that. He's good for you."

"Maybe." That was all she was willing to concede at the moment. "I missed calls from Wade and Jess as well. Are they calling me to tell me the same thing?"

"Probably. Mom was calling all of us tonight."

"Thanks for the warning, big brother."

"No problem. Just make sure I get the biggest slice of wedding cake."

Kelsi ended the call, turning to Shane. "My mom is calling my brothers. And my cousin. I'm sure that she's trying to get people here to pressure me to marry Bobby as well."

"So what are you going to do about it?" he asked.

"I'm going to think. I'll figure something out by tomorrow, I'm sure."

"Something like how wonderful it would be to be the local sheriff's wife?"

Kelsi groaned. "That's one option, isn't it?"

"It is." He frowned at her. "You're really upset about this, aren't you?"

She nodded. "Mom and Dad are expecting us to do everything they say right now. I might really get pressure from the others to marry Bobby."

"Let me drive," he said, getting out to walk around to the passenger side. "I'm not sure you should drive upset."

"I just feel like my life is spiraling out of control!" she said, obediently scooting across to the passenger seat. "I'm not sure what to do!"

"Well, you know what *I* think you should do," he said, grinning over at her.

"And if I decide I'm bored and uninterested in you in two weeks? Then what will you say?"

"I'll know I need to step up my game. It's my job to be sure I don't bore you. I'll make sure we get date nights. I'll take you out and teach you to shoot."

Kelsi perked up at that. "You will? Can I get a lavender gun?"

"Why do you need a lavender gun?"

"Because even self-defense accessories should be pretty!"

He groaned, running his fingers through his hair before starting the truck. "They should? What about my gun for work?"

"Oh, loan it to me for an hour. I'll get it all blinged up for you!"

"*Blinged up*? The bad guys will laugh me out of town."

"What bad guys? You're the sheriff of Riston, Idaho where the most exciting thing that ever happens is old

Jaclyn Hardy gets scared and kills one of her lawn gnomes with a hoe in the middle of the night!"

Shane laughed. "That was hilarious! How long has she managed the RV park on the ranch for your family?" He hadn't been amused when he'd been called out of bed by one of the guests at the ranch, but in retrospect, it was hilarious.

"Honestly, I have no idea. I remember going to her house when I was a little girl and playing with her bunnies, so it's been a really long time."

"Why exactly does she have so many rabbits?"

"She said she's too unique to be a crazy cat lady, so she's going to be the best reality-challenged bunny lady around." Kelsi shrugged. "As far as I can tell, she's the only bunny lady around, reality-challenged or not. She's always been one of my favorite people."

"I heard she talks to the gnomes. Is that true?"

"Never!" Kelsi responded, sounding offended at the accusation.

"Oh, good. I was worried she wasn't sane enough to be on her own."

"She only talks to the fairies and the leprechauns. She said the gnomes are too stuck up for the likes of her, so she ignores them for the most part."

"Does she have a psychiatrist?"

"As far as I know, she hasn't left the ranch in twenty years. She has everything she needs brought to her, or she goes to the general store onsite to buy it." She shrugged. "She doesn't hurt anyone, and we all love her. I think she should be left alone."

"You should talk to her about Bobby Blakely. Maybe she'll give you good advice."

Kelsi sighed. "She was Grandma Kelsey's best friend when they were young, and when Grandma married

Granddad and moved here, Jaclyn was part of the package. She really played a big role in my up-bringing. Every time I got too mad at my siblings, I'd declare a bunny day and go to live with her. I never lasted more than an hour or two, because when I got there, she'd make me start cleaning the bunnies' litter boxes. I hated that job!"

He laughed softly. "Which is why you always got it, I'm sure!"

"She also would make snickerdoodles, and every time I visited her, she would give me milk and snickerdoodles, and she would serve it all on this fancy tea set. I always felt so grown up at her house."

"Go talk to her then. I'm sure she'll have good advice for you."

"Or she might just send me on errands. She does that sometimes!" Kelsi shrugged. "Either way, I'll go talk to her tomorrow."

"What are your big plans for your day off?"

"I'll sleep until seven, which is like manna from heaven for me, go to town for church at nine. After church, I'll come home and do my laundry, which is my favorite part of the weekend, and then I'll go see Jaclyn and chat with her. It's been a couple of weeks, and I like to make sure she's okay."

"I'm glad you still have her. It sounds like you miss your grandmother a lot."

She nodded emphatically. "I do. She was my strength. I think I always felt extra close to her because of the name thing, but I'm not sure if that's all it was. Dani and I looked just like she did, except for the eyes. I used to stare at her wedding pictures, and know I'd look like that one day, and be filled with pride that I looked like her."

"And do you? Look like her that is?"

"Exactly. It's funny, but I was always one of the tallest

kids in school. Mom would say that we were going to be as tall as the pine trees, but we both stopped growing in fifth grade when we were the same height as Grandma Kelsey. She'd just pat us and say, 'There's a whole lot of wonderful packed into that height.' Dani loved her too. Dani and I were really close when we were little."

"What happened?"

Kelsi shrugged. "It's not that we're not close now. I love her. We just kind of grew apart. We didn't like being dressed identically all the time, so we were thrilled when we could start wearing whatever we wanted to wear. She wanted to dress more…casually, I guess is the best word. I enjoyed dressing up and being a little more feminine. So we kind of grew apart in every way. I think she just wanted to be Dani instead of Kelsianddani. For years our names were all one word. Or worse yet. The twins. One of our teachers couldn't tell us apart, so she just called us both twin. She'd point at one of us and say, 'What do you think, twin?' We tried correcting her for the first month, but it became obvious she just didn't care. We were two halves of a whole for way too long."

"That's sad. I'm glad you two still get along though. It would be awful if people behaving like that ruined your relationship with your sister." Shane pulled onto the road leading to the café and the ranch house.

"Let's just stop at the café so you can get your truck." She knew he'd feel obligated to see her home, because she knew that's the kind of man he was.

"Nah. I'll walk back to my truck after taking you home." He drove past the café and parked in the parking lot on the other side of the ranch house from the highway. "The parking lot of the café is too lit up at night. I don't feel like I can kiss you goodnight there. Not in a way that will make your toes curl anyway."

She made a face at that. "You always think you have to make my toes curl."

"I do have to make your toes curl. You have such pretty little toes."

Kelsi raised an eyebrow at him. "And why have you noticed my toes?"

"You sometimes wear sandals to church in the summer. I notice everything about you, Kelsi Weston."

"You do, do you? I notice everything about you too, Sheriff Shane."

"You do not. You didn't even know where I lived!"

"So? Your house isn't you. I notice *you*. You're wearing a new shirt today, and I like it. The blue and brown plaid bring out your eyes. Do you have any idea how much I love your eyes? They always make me feel like I'm drowning in a giant vat of chocolate."

"Oh, and I know you like chocolate."

"You show me a woman who doesn't like chocolate, and I'll show you one who really did have her taste buds burned off. Chocolate is the only reason for getting up in the mornings! Chocolate is better than anything!"

He laughed. "I will bring you some chocolate." He unbuckled and scooted toward her on the truck seat. "What are you doing tomorrow evening? Can I see you?"

She wrinkled her nose. "Tomorrow night is family dinner at the café, and it's my turn to cook."

"Want some help?" He had no idea why, but he wanted to be there for her family dinner. He wanted all of them to accept him as her future, whether they really believed he would be part of it or not.

She tilted her head to one side and finally nodded. "Sure. I was planning on cooking lasagna and making a salad and garlic bread to go with it. Does that sound good? With a family as big as mine, I always feel like I should make enough for an Italian family, so I tend to make lots of Italian."

"You realize that makes no sense, don't you?"

She shrugged. "Making sense all the time is a sign of a boring brain."

"I'll keep that in mind. I can meet you at the café at four maybe? What time is dinner?"

"We usually eat at six. Meet me at four-thirty. That'll be enough time to get everything ready." She reached for him, wrapping her arms around his neck. "Thanks for a wonderful day and for not laughing at my quest for Bigfoot. We'll find him someday."

He grinned, leaning down to brush her lips with his. "And when we do, we need to get him to pose for pictures, so you can prove to your brothers you were right all along."

"And Dani. And Jess, who hasn't been quite as bad as the others about the whole Bigfoot thing, but she was still annoying."

"How was she annoying?"

"She was always too busy to go with me!" Kelsi complained. "A cousin who loved me would have been willing to search for Bigfoot every weekend!"

He grinned, pulling her against him for another kiss. "We'll prove them all wrong. Dream of me."

She sighed, stroking his cheek. "How could I do anything else?" She slipped out of the truck and went into the house, her mind racing. He was different than Donn, that was for sure. But how could she know if she could make a marriage work with him? She had to get her mother off her back about Bobby, because once her siblings all started to put pressure on her to not make her mother angry, she wasn't sure if she could stand strong.

Maybe marrying Shane right away *was* the best idea.

When she closed her eyes that night, she pictured herself and Shane in the mouse ears like he'd mentioned, and she had a smile on her face. He was a good man, and he loved her. Would it be so wrong to marry him before she was sure of her own feelings?

Chapter Six

AFTER FINISHING her laundry the next day, Kelsi made the fifteen minute walk from the ranch house across the ranch to the small cabin where Jaclyn Hardy lived. She was excited to see her old friend and wished she took more time to stop and see her. The older woman had no family, other than Kelsi and her siblings, so one of them should be checking on her more often than once a week.

Kelsi made her way through the army of gnomes, leprechauns, and fairies that cavorted in the yard. They looked like they'd recently been scrubbed clean, which wouldn't surprise her one little bit. Jaclyn had always preferred her army of outdoor fantasy creatures to people.

She knocked on the door and immediately heard a yell in response. "Keep your pants on! I'm coming!" When the door was flung open, Jaclyn's eyes grew wide as she smiled. "If it isn't my favorite Weston child! To what do I owe this pleasure?" She opened her door wide, inviting Kelsi to come in.

As soon as she stepped into the house, one of the bunnies hopped across her foot, and Kelsi squatted down to pat its head. "I don't think I've seen you before. What's your name?"

"The bunnies don't talk, you know. They're not stuck up like the gnomes, but they're kind of stupid," Jaclyn told her. "I'm going to get our tea ready. You want milk or actual tea this time?"

Now that she was an adult, the older woman always gave her a choice of beverage, but Kelsi wanted things to be like they'd always been. "I'd like milk please."

"Well, sit down. I'll be back in a moment, and we'll chat about whatever has your mind so clouded."

Kelsi looked around the room, and smiled at the familiarity. Everything stayed the same there, except the color of the bunnies. She knew that none of the rabbits had ever come from a pet store. The first had been injured, and Jaclyn had nursed it back to life. Then she'd found another and brought it in.

With the speed of the rabbits procreating, and the addition of more over the years, the older woman usually had between twenty and thirty bunnies in her house at all times.

When Jaclyn came back with the tea, she put it on the coffee table, pouring her tea into a cup, and handing Kelsi her milk. "Snickerdoodle?" she asked, offering the plate.

"I would love a snickerdoodle." Kelsi took two, putting them on the small plate Jaclyn provided. She knew how much Jaclyn loved her rituals where tea was concerned.

"Talk to me about what's happening, Kelsi. I can see by your eyes that you have a dilemma and, fitting for your age, it's centered around men. Three of them, I think?"

Kelsi sighed, wondering how Jaclyn always knew what she was thinking. "Well, you know I've been dating Donn for a long time..."

"Donn was an idiot. If he's the first one, cross him off

your list. You should have gotten rid of that boy seven years ago."

"Yes, ma'am," Kelsi answered automatically, knowing Jaclyn was right. "The second man is Sheriff Shane."

"Oh! I know Sheriff Shane! He was the one who came to check on me after I clobbered poor George to death, thinking he was a snake." Jaclyn sniffled. "I miss George."

Kelsi patted the older woman's hand. "That's right. Well, as soon as Donn left town, the sheriff asked me out. We've seen each other several times, and I have to admit, I'm developing feelings for him."

"Shane's a good man. Strong. He'd be a good husband for you. You'd have strong, beautiful babies together."

Kelsi blushed, not quite ready to think about the babies she might have with the sheriff. "The third man is a boy I knew in elementary school who my mother met on her travels. He's a cook now, and since the café just lost its cook…"

"Did that good-for-nothing Kathy finally find a rich guest to run off with?" Jaclyn asked, shaking her head as she peered at Kelsi over her teacup.

Kelsi nodded. She was always amazed by what Jaclyn knew when she never left the ranch. There seemed to be no local gossip the woman wasn't privy to. She wondered if her informant was the same as her mother's. "She did, and now Bobby is coming back to cook for the café, which is good in one way, because I don't have to find someone."

"And that sister of yours doesn't need to be around people any more than necessary," Jaclyn said, shaking her head.

"Very true! I don't want him here though. Mother thinks I need to marry him, and she's started calling my siblings and telling them to put pressure on me to marry Bobby when he gets here. All I remember about Bobby is he was annoying and chased Dani and me around the playground at recess with snakes and lizards."

"Oh, *that* Bobby. I remember him. No, you're better off without that boy. The sheriff is the one for you," Jaclyn spoke with an air of authority, as if she could see all the men and knew what Kelsi needed.

Kelsi sighed. "I think so too, but I get bored with men so quickly."

Jaclyn shook her head vehemently. "You've gotten bored with the *boys* you've dated. Sheriff Shane is very much a man. You won't get bored with him."

"I'm not in love with him. At least I don't think I am."

"Of course you're not. You've only been dating a few days. You will be in love with him, though. Sheriff Shane is your soul mate."

"What makes you say that?" Kelsi asked, startled.

Jaclyn shrugged, her dress loose on her thin shoulders. "I knew it the moment I met him. There was just something about his face that told me he was meant for you. I wanted to tell you so many times, but I knew I had to save that information for the right day for you to believe me. Today is that day."

Kelsi frowned, wishing she knew what to say. "He's asked me to marry him, so I don't have to put up with Mom's matchmaking."

"And you're trying to decide if it would be fair to marry him, when he's obviously so in love with you, and you don't know how you feel yet."

"You've always been able to know what I'm thinking."

Jaclyn smiled, looking down at one of the bunnies. "The fairies tell me a lot of things," she finally said. "Yes, you need to marry the sheriff, and you need to do it this week. Sunday would be the best day. Would you like me to come?"

Kelsi gaped at the older woman. "The *fairies* told you I need to marry the sheriff on Sunday?" The fairies were being awfully particular lately.

"You look for Bigfoot every chance you get, and you question my connection with the fairies? *Really*?"

Kelsi choked back a laugh. How could she possibly respond to that? "I would like you to come, but I have to tell the sheriff, if I do decide I want to marry him, first."

"Of course you do. Who wouldn't want to marry that huge hunk of hotness? If I were fifty years younger, I'd be all over him, demanding he make an honest woman of me."

"Are you dishonest now?"

"Every woman deserves her secrets!"

"They do." Kelsi finished her milk and snickerdoodles. "I'm glad we had this chat."

"So are the fairies. They've been worried about you."

"So has my mother!" Kelsi grinned. "Let me help you clean up before I head back to the house. Do you need anything before I go?"

"I'm not an old woman who needs someone to take care of her! You just send word when the wedding is, and I'll be there." Jaclyn got up and bustled around, putting the dishes into the sink.

Kelsi smiled, catching the old woman by surprise by kissing her cheek. "I'll come see you again soon."

Jaclyn smiled, raising her hand in a wave. "Listen to the fairies now!"

"Yes, ma'am!"

* * *

Kelsi was at the café at four-thirty with all the ingredients for the meal she planned to cook. She opened the door that led straight to the kitchen and put the groceries on the counter before walking over to unlock the front door, so the others could join her when they arrived. She was a bit surprised Shane wasn't there yet, and wondered what had held him up.

Her mind played her conversation with Jaclyn over and over, thinking about what she'd said. Despite her belief that she could hear fairies, Kelsi knew the older woman was smart, and her Grandma Kelsey had always had great respect for her. She'd always told her if she wasn't around, she should listen to Jaclyn.

Shane was a few minutes later than he meant to be, and he stopped in the doorway of the kitchen, leaned against the wall and just watched Kelsi work. She obviously had her mind on something else, and he didn't want to startle her.

"Do you have any idea how beautiful you look, standing there, making dinner for your family?"

Kelsi looked up at him and smiled, her eyes sparkling. "I went and saw Jaclyn today."

"She didn't try to bash you over the head with a hoe, did she?"

"No, but she did say that you were very kind to her after she killed poor George that night."

"George? Are all those gnomes in her yard named?"

Kelsi nodded. "Do you believe? All the gnomes, fairies, leprechauns, and bunnies have names. I'm doing good to remember the names of my breasts!"

He blinked a few times. "Your breasts have names?"

"Don't everyone's?"

He decided that trying to follow her line of reasoning would just take him further down the rabbit hole, so he let it go. "What else did Jaclyn say?"

"She said she knew the first time that she met you that

you were my soul mate, and I need to forget about Donn and Bobby, and marry you next Sunday. She's willing to come to the wedding, so we need to give her plenty of notice."

He blinked a few times before grinning. "How did she know that I was your soul mate?"

"It was either something in your face or the fairies told her. It was hard to keep up with the conversation at times."

"So are you going to take her advice?" he asked.

Kelsi frowned. "I'm thinking about it. Grandma Kelsey always said if she wasn't around I should go to Jaclyn. They were best friends their whole lives, you see."

"Really? You're considering it?"

"I wouldn't say I was if I wasn't. Do you think I'm the kind of girl who would give a man false hope?"

He smiled, sticking his hand into the front pocket of his jeans, before walking toward her. "I got you something today."

She made a face. "What? It's not a lizard, is it?"

"Why would I get you a lizard?" he asked, surprised she'd even worry about something like that.

"I guess I still have Bobby Blakely on my mind."

Shane shook his head. "Not a lizard, and you shouldn't think about other men when you're with me, you know." He caught one of her hands in his, frowning down at the tomato on it. "You should wash your hands."

She frowned at him. "I'm making supper. They'll just get dirty again!"

"Would you wash them? *Please?*"

She rolled her eyes and walked to the sink, washing her hands and drying them with the towel she'd laid out earlier. "There. My hands are clean. Want to hold them now?"

He took her hand in his again and quickly dropped to one knee. "Kelsi, will you do me the honor of being my wife? If we marry on Sunday, we'll make the fairies happy!"

Kelsi stared down at him and the ring he held poised to put on her finger. "Where'd you get that?" she asked, recognizing it.

"Will gave it to me. He said your grandmother had left it with him when she knew she was dying, instructing that he make sure you had it as your engagement ring."

Kelsi swiped a tear from her eye. Grandma Kelsey's engagement ring. He cared enough to use Grandma Kelsey's ring. She stared down at him for a minute, her mind racing. She wasn't sure if it was the right thing to do, because she didn't know if she loved him yet, but with Bobby on his way, and the pressure she'd surely receive from her family, it might be their only chance.

Finally, she nodded, and he slipped the ring on her finger. Getting to his feet, he swept her into a kiss. "I'm going to make you the happiest woman alive!"

"I know you are." She rested her head on his shoulder for a moment. "You promised you'd helped me find Bigfoot."

He groaned. "I'm going to regret that, aren't I?"

She shrugged, looking down at the ring, which fit her finger perfectly. "You are." Standing on tiptoe, she kissed his cheek. "I have to get back to work. Do you want to get the garlic bread ready?"

He nodded, hurrying over to wash his hands while his heart rejoiced. She was going to marry him. He'd asked and asked, but he hadn't believed she'd really agree. He'd have to go see Jaclyn and thank her and all her fairy friends.

They worked together in silence, but when they had to reach past each other, there was always a loving stroke along an arm or a quick kiss. She smiled, pleased with him.

Never had she dated someone she wanted to *touch* as much as him.

It was shortly before six when the noise from the front of the café started. Dani was there first, and she walked back to check on the preparations. Her eyes, so like Kelsi's, showed no surprise when she saw him standing in the kitchen. "You joining us for supper?"

He nodded. "If you don't mind, that is?"

Dani shrugged. "I don't hate you." Her eyes went to her sister. "Need any help?"

Kelsi shook her head. "I have my short-order sheriff here. He's a good kitchen-lackey. You go collapse in one of the booths until the boys get here. You look exhausted!"

Dani yawned, hiding it behind her hand. "I'm pretty tired. They worked us hard." She wandered out of the kitchen.

"You didn't tell her we're getting married!" he said, frowning at Kelsi.

"I'm going to tell the whole family together," she answered quickly. "Trust me, it'll be easier that way."

"You know your family better than I do!"

"God love them all," she muttered. She wasn't looking forward to their dinner, because she knew her brothers had all talked to their mother about Bobby. Why she felt guilty for not wanting to marry a stranger, she'd never know, but her mother could make people feel guilty for saving the world.

Jess was the next to arrive. Jess was going to school to be a veterinarian, and her life wasn't as entwined in running the ranch as the others. She did make it to every family dinner, though. Their cousin had the trademark Weston ice blue eyes that all the siblings shared. The eyes were the one way the twins hadn't looked like their grandma.

"Need any help?" she asked Kelsi, openly staring at the sheriff.

Kelsi shook her head. "Shane and I have it."

"Why's he here? You never invited Donn."

"Donn The Doofus didn't deserve an invite. I'm here because Kelsi and I are dating," Shane responded.

"Okay." Jess shrugged. "I'll go wait for everyone. I might borrow a page from Dani's book and nap."

One-by-one, the brothers came in, and the café got louder and louder. Will was the only one to stick his head in the back. "Hey, Shane. Kelsi."

"Hey, Will. Tell everyone five more minutes!"

Her brother nodded, looking back and forth between them, before heading back out. "Kelsi says five more minutes."

Kelsi put food on plates, and Shane carried it out to everyone. He couldn't figure out why everyone let her do all the work, but he figured there must be a system. Kelsi was not a woman to let her family take advantage of her without putting up a fight.

When they were all sitting around two of the four tops pushed together, Kelsi looked up and down the table at the people she loved the most. "I know everyone is wondering why Shane is here."

"I heard you were dating at the same time that I heard you fought with Will in the restaurant on Monday night," Wade said. "Don't do that again."

Wyatt just looked at them, nodding politely.

Wesley, her rock-climbing brother, frowned at her. He led the more difficult excursions into the mountains. "Mom wants you to marry Bobby. He's coming up here to take over the kitchen. Why are you dating Shane?"

Kelsi took a deep breath. "I was dating Shane before Mom decided I should marry Bobby. And I'm going to marry Shane. He asked me tonight." She held up her hand with the ring on it. Only Will and Dani didn't look surprised.

Dani nodded at her, a slight smile on her lips. Kelsi understood. They may emphasize their differences by dressing differently and wearing their hair as different as they could, but they were still twins, and they still had a connection that was special.

"Wait!" Wade frowned. "Isn't that Grandma Kelsey's ring?"

Will nodded. "Absolutely. Grandma Kelsey gave it to me shortly before she died and told me to give it to a man Kelsi dated who was worthy of marrying her. Shane is."

"We're getting married Sunday," Kelsi said over the mumbling of her family. "With me or against me, it's happening, so you might as well be onboard."

The brothers looked at each other before Wade, the oldest and the manager of the whole of River's End Ranch, stood and walked to Kelsi, pulling her out of her chair and into his hug. All four of the brothers made Dani and Kelsi look like Lilliputians. "I'm happy for you!"

Kelsi smiled, knowing that having Wade's seal of approval would make all the other brothers immediately fall in line.

Wade looked down at Shane, offering his hand to shake. "Welcome to the family. Make her happy, or we'll kill you." The words were said with a slight smile on his face, but Shane had no doubt he meant them.

"I'll do my very best."

The enthusiasm that greeted Shane then, with hugs and back pats and handshakes, was a bit overwhelming. Even if his family *had* been the size of Kelsi's, they were more laid back and didn't often get riled up about anything. He could see he had some adjusting to do, but he'd do it gladly. For Kelsi. He'd do anything for her.

After they'd finished eating, Kelsi and Shane left, walking along the grass. Kelsi took a deep breath of the spring air, feeling engaged for the first time since he'd slid the ring on her finger. "I'm glad Wade welcomed you like he did. I don't know if the other brothers would have otherwise."

"Will already did when I talked to him earlier."

Kelsi looked down at her hand, the diamond in the ring glinting a bit by the light of the moon. "I'm nervous but happy all at once. We're getting married, Shane!" She loved the idea of spending her life with him, but was it just the newness of dating him? Would it wear off?

"Is your mother going to fly back to try to talk you out of it?"

She shook her head. "Nope. Because all my siblings agreed to keep it quiet. We're going to have a small, private, secret wedding at the ranch house next Sunday."

"When did they agree to keep it quiet?"

She smiled. "Dani went around and asked them all for me."

"Dani? I didn't see you two talk about it!"

Kelsi shrugged. "Sometimes we don't have to. We have the twin connection-thing going. Sometimes we are so far apart mentally, it's like we were raised in different countries, and then there are moments, like tonight, where we just click, and she reads my mind and we make things happen."

"Am I allowed to talk about the wedding?"

She shrugged. "I'd rather you didn't. Get Pastor Randy to agree to marry us, and we'll get our marriage license in Post Falls. Then no one in town will know except Pastor Randy, and you swear him to secrecy." She shook her head. "Mom has a spy in town, and we have no idea who it is, so we can't be seen planning the wedding. She'll do a lot better hearing about it after the fact.

"How did you figure all this out so quickly?"

"I was thinking about how I'd make it work after talking to Jaclyn today. I need to take you by one day this week, so we can invite her to our wedding. She'll assign the fairies to help us keep it quiet."

Shane didn't argue. Instead, he slipped his arm around her, and stopped at a park bench in front of the lake. "How did we get all the way to the lake?" he asked, surprised.

She shrugged. "When you asked me to go for a walk, I immediately headed this way. I always walk down to the lake when I'm sad or happy...or just need to be away from the chaos that is my family. It's kind of my place."

"Works for me." He sat on the bench, pulling her down close to him. "One week from today, you're going to be my wife."

Kelsi grinned, stroking his cheek. "I know."

"I'm just bragging a little bit," he told her. "I can't tell anyone else, so I'll just keep telling you over and over."

She laughed softly, resting her head on his shoulder. "You should ask Will to be your best man."

"Will? Is he your favorite brother?"

"He's the brother I'm closest to. I never thought we'd both make it to adulthood alive, because I was sure one of us would kill the other, but we're really close. I promise."

"I figured that when he was the one who had the ring. He called me today, you know."

She pulled away and looked at him with surprise. "No, I didn't know. What did he say?"

"He told me that he thought we should get married quick so that your Mother didn't ruin things, and then he said he had something that would help me if I wanted to come get it." Shane kissed the tip of her nose. "We talked for a couple of hours. That's why I was late getting to the café to see you. He made sure he gave me the 'be good to our baby sister' speech before he gave me the ring."

She looked down at the object in question, feeling the unusual weight on her finger. "I'm glad to have it. I wondered where it had gone when she stopped wearing it a few weeks before she died, but every time I asked, she changed the subject. She had a different diamond ring that disappeared about the same time that I bet one of our brothers has for Dani."

"Which brother?"

Kelsi shrugged. "Probably Wyatt, but Dani's a lot more private than I am. We're so much alike physically, but so different in other ways."

"I'm glad you said you'd marry me. I hope you know that I'm going to make sure you're happy."

She smiled. "I just hope I can do the same for you."

Shane shook his head with a smile. "Don't you know you've already done that, just by agreeing?"

Chapter Seven

Kelsi wore the ring on a chain around her neck the following day, so her mother's informant wouldn't find out about the wedding. She knew she was probably being over-dramatic about it, but her mother was a force to be reckoned with, and it wasn't a reckoning she wanted for her wedding day.

When Shane came into the café, she watched to see if what he'd said was true, and sure enough, the other waitresses didn't acknowledge him at all. She hurried over and leaned down to kiss his cheek, before sliding into the booth across from him. "Hi!"

He grinned at her. "Hi." Taking her hand in his, he frowned down at it. "Where's the ring? Don't you like it? I'll buy a different one if you don't want to wear your grandmother's."

She pulled the ring out from under her shirt and showed it to him. "I'm worried about Mom's spy."

He shook his head. "Really? Her spy? Is she the head of the CIA or something?" Why would her mother have spies?

Kelsi shook her head, leaning forward to whisper, "Every move I've made since she left, she's known about. She knew I broke up with Donn and that we lost a cook, and I know none of my siblings told her. I feel like there are spies everywhere!" She looked around the café for cameras. "Just for this one week, we have to keep it quiet. After the wedding, we'll tell everyone."

He sighed, shaking his head at her. "And you're willing to have a small wedding without everyone you love to make sure she doesn't find out?"

"Yes!" Kelsi sighed. "Now, I found Grandma Kelsey's wedding dress, which she'd carefully saved for Dani and me. It's in perfect condition, and it fits. It's like it was made for me. So I'm wearing that. Dani is going to wear a dress I have that will accent her eyes. I think that stuff is settled. What about you, Sheriff? What are you going to wear?"

He shrugged. "I have a black suit. Will that work?" He was more worried about getting her down the aisle than what either of them would wear.

She nodded. "Have you ordered the mouse ears?"

"I have. They'll be here Friday." His thumb brushed over her palm. "Have you stopped to tell Jaclyn about the wedding yet?" He wanted to go with her to see the older woman, if she didn't mind. Without Jaclyn, he wasn't sure she'd be marrying him so quickly.

"No. I haven't had a chance. Do you want to go with me?"

His eyes lit up. "I can't think of anything I'd like more! She makes me laugh."

"Well, meet me here around three, and I'll be ready to take off." She scooted out of the booth. "So what can I get for you today, Sheriff?"

"Other than you?"

She made a face. "You've already got *me*. What do you want to eat?"

He noticed she was still wearing the red boots she'd borrowed from her sister. "When are you going to give those back?"

She looked down at them with a grin. "I think I'm just going to buy her a new pair. Won't these look great with my wedding dress?" She loved the idea of wearing the red boots with the pretty dress. It would put her own spin on things.

"Sure!" Were women supposed to wear red cowboy boots with wedding dresses? He wasn't sure, but he wouldn't argue with her. "Just a burger today, I think."

She nodded and hurried off, already knowing how he wanted the burger. How could she not after years of serving him every day?

* * *

When Shane got to Kelsey's Kafé a few hours later, he walked around back, knowing she'd have the kitchen door unlocked for him. He slipped in the door and found her starting the dishwasher.

"I'm ready," she said over her shoulder, sensing his presence more than hearing him. The dishwasher was already too loud for her to be able to hear the door open.

He walked up behind her and wrapped his arms around her waist, hugging her tightly. "I missed you today."

She patted his hand, turning in his arms to encircle his neck with her own arms. "I missed you too. You're starting to get under my skin, Sheriff."

"Good. Because you've been under mine for years." He

dropped a kiss on her forehead. "You ready to go tell Jaclyn?"

She nodded emphatically. "She's going to be so happy."

"I hope the fairies are happy too. What do we do if the gnomes are mad?" He knew she didn't find the whole spectrum of mythical creatures as amusing as he did, but she was usually willing to joke with him about them.

"No idea!" she responded. "I don't think Jaclyn cares about the gnomes opinions too much." She took his hand and pulled him toward the back door, locking up as they went. "I got us both four-wheelers, because I thought it would be fun if we went down by the lake as well." A picnic on a cool spring evening with a special man sounded like heaven. She'd never wanted to do things like that with Donn, and as his name popped into her head, she realized she didn't miss him at all. After an eight-year relationship, she probably should, but she couldn't.

He shrugged, standing next to one of the four-wheelers and putting the black helmet on his head. "Sounds good to me."

She held up a bag. "I packed us a picnic dinner. Race you!"

Before he had a chance to throw a leg over the four-wheeler to get on, she was gone.

She'd swerved around the building and was out of sight before he even got his four-wheeler started. He should have known she'd cheat, but of course, he'd had no idea they would race, so how could he have prepared? She was the most competitive woman he'd ever met in his life. He wouldn't be surprised to see her have a contest to see who could grow their hair faster.

He loved driving across the ranch. He could see so much more this way than he ever had by sticking to the roads with his police vehicle. Growing up in a place that was so full of beauty and so unpopulated must have been wonderful.

By the time Shane was parked amidst the fantasy creatures in Jaclyn's yard, Kelsi was already standing at the door. He walked up behind her, placed a hand at her waist, and leaned down to whisper, "You cheated!"

"In my family, if you don't cheat, you're not trying hard enough!"

He shook his head, smiling down at Jaclyn as she opened her door. "Well if it isn't the newly-engaged couple. Come in for tea!" She opened her door wide, a silent invitation for them both to enter.

Kelsi grinned stepping inside. "Milk for me, please."

Jaclyn looked at Shane. "Do you want milk or tea with your snickerdoodles?"

"Tea, please."

"Sit! Both of you! The fairies told me you were coming, so I have the tea already made."

Shane sat on the couch, a perplexed look on his face. "The fairy thing creeps me out a little."

"She's awesome. Deal with it," Kelsi hissed back.

Jaclyn was there a moment later with a tea tray laden with cookies. Once they had all been served, she sat in an armchair perpendicular to the couch and patted Jaclyn's arm. "I'm glad you followed my advice. What time is the wedding on Sunday?"

Kelsi looked over at Shane. "Have you talked to the pastor?"

He nodded. "Yeah, wedding is at four. He said that gives him time to eat lunch and nap after Sunday service."

Kelsi sighed happily. "Naps are made of awesome!" She often took a quick nap after she got off work in the afternoon, because she was up so early. She hated going to bed at eight, because it made her feel like a child with an early bedtime.

"The wedding will be in the backyard of the main house. Do you want one of my brothers to come get you?"

Jaclyn made a face. "Why would I need one of your brothers to come get me? I'm just old, not sick."

"I thought I'd offer." Kelsi took a bite of one of her cookies. "Snickerdoodles are particularly good today."

Shane looked between the two women, feeling a little out of place in the feminine surroundings. Everything was draped with pink, and it reminded him a bit of Pepto Bismol. "How are the bunnies, Miss Hardy?"

"The same as always, and don't you worry. I haven't killed any of my gnomes since George. That's not something I do often."

"Yes, ma'am. Thank you for talking to Kelsi about marrying me. I think it was your advice that made her agree." He wouldn't bring up George's untimely death, because he knew the woman was embarrassed about killing a lawn ornament. "I'm *sure* it was. She was dragging her feet every time I asked before you told her what the fairies said."

"Why don't you believe in the fairies?" Jaclyn asked, her eyes level on his. "They're ancient creatures who have been around much longer than humans. They're here to help us all."

Shane wasn't certain how to respond. "I've never seen a fairy, Miss Hardy. I guess I'm one of those men who needs to see to believe."

"You miss out on so much that way. Do you believe in love?" Jaclyn asked. "You can't see that either."

Shane looked at Kelsi. "Oh, but I can. I really can."

Kelsi blushed under his gaze. It felt so strange having him openly talk about loving her when she didn't yet know how she felt. How exactly was she supposed to react? She patted his arm, lost for words.

Jaclyn laughed. "You overwhelm her with your feelings, Sheriff. She never thought anyone would love her quite the way you do."

Kelsi quickly gulped down her milk and stood. "I think we should be off now. We're having a picnic by the lake, and we need to have our four-wheelers back before dark."

Jaclyn tilted her head to the side, looking at the younger woman. "That's not a ranch rule, and I think everyone in this room knows it. You just want to get away so I don't mention how embarrassed you are again."

Kelsi shrugged, grabbing Shane's hand. He put down his tea and got to his feet. "Thank you for the tea and cookies."

Jaclyn got to her feet, smiling, her blue eyes dancing with laughter. "So happy to have you both. I'll see you Sunday. I'll be the one wearing fairy wings."

"Fairy wings?" Shane asked as soon as they were a short distance from the small house. "Is she really going to wear fairy wings to our wedding?"

"As long as she wears *something*, I'll be happy."

Shane laughed, getting onto his four-wheeler. "Where do you want to picnic?" he asked.

Kelsi shrugged. "Wherever. Maybe down on the other side of the lake. I haven't been there since the snow melted, and there might be some signs." She didn't really feel like doing anything but spending time with him, but she'd mention her search to keep him from getting a big head. No one needed a big-headed sheriff for a husband.

He nodded, knowing it was going to turn into a hunt for Bigfoot, and started his four-wheeler, ready to follow her anywhere.

When they got to a small grassy area to the south of

the lake, he removed his helmet, watching her closely. "That whole thing with Jaclyn made you uncomfortable, didn't it?"

She nodded. "I just feel like I'm doing something wrong by marrying you when I know you love me, and I don't yet return your feelings."

He took the blanket she'd tied to the back of his vehicle and spread it out on the ground. "The word *yet* is what I'm counting on. I truly believe the feelings will come." At least he hoped they would. He knew there was electricity between them, and for now that would have to do.

He sat and waited as she put the sandwiches she'd made on the blanket. "I'm not hungry yet," she said quietly. "The cookies were enough to keep me going for a while."

"Do you want to talk then? Or do you want to look for signs of Bigfoot?" He dangled the opportunity to search for her favorite beast over her head like a carrot stick.

Kelsi sighed. "As much as I want to talk Bigfoot, we should probably talk future instead. We're getting married Sunday, you know."

He smiled, taking her hand in his. "I am aware of this plan."

"So do you want kids or not?" she asked, as if it had been the topic of conversation all along.

He shrugged. "I would like at least one or two? What about you?"

"Oh, I'd cover the ranch with kids if I thought I could. I've always wanted at least a dozen."

He swallowed hard. "A dozen? Really?" He couldn't imagine having a family that big.

"Do you think that's too many?" she asked, frowning at him. "There were six in my family, and sometimes I wish there'd been more."

"But your siblings make you crazy!"

"They do. But they also fight for me and keep me going. They're the people who balance me and keep me on the right track. They tease me all day, but if someone else teases me, they're the first to make them stop. They have my back no matter what."

"I can see that, but isn't having the five of them—six if you count Jess—enough? I mean that's a lot of people."

She shrugged. "The more, the merrier. Don't you think you want more siblings?"

"It's not really that way with my sister and me. We're not as close." He sighed. "I don't care how many kids we have. As long as we can afford them."

"Okay, I promised Wade I'd talk to you about something. You know the ranch isn't ours, right? We're still playing games and jumping through hoops to get our hands on it. Mom and Dad are going to be giving us a test, and we have no idea what it is, but we have to pass their test to be able to get our hands on the ranch."

"You don't think I'm marrying you for the potential income from the ranch, do you?" he asked, his eyes wide. He thought he'd made it very clear that his interest was in her, not in her family's wealth.

"No, I don't. If I did, I wouldn't be marrying you, no matter what the fairies said!" She grinned at him. "I needed to make sure you understood the financial situation for Wade. I'm paid a salary, and it's a decent salary, but I'm about to give up the free housing that comes with it." She frowned. "Which is another thing we haven't talked about! I assume you want me to live in town with you?"

He nodded. "I'll even make room on my DVD shelf for you to put your slasher movies on."

"I'm sure they'll look good on display in your living room." She moved a little closer to him, pressing a kiss to his cheek. "I'm not going to have a lot of time this week. I have packing to do, and little details to see to. The restaurant here on property is catering the wedding for us, and I'm going to have tables set up on the lawn. It's such a beautiful time of year, so if it doesn't rain, we're doing everything outdoors. If it does rain, we probably will need to move to the café."

"Why don't you guys have a building for huge events? I would think, with as much as you have going on here, you'd have something set up for weddings."

She shrugged. "I'm not sure. River's End has always been a place to go to do stuff...not to stay inside and have dances. It's been all about experiencing the beauty of nature in your own way. Whether you like snow or summer, there's something wonderful for you to do here. I think Granddad always thought that if we had a reception area, people would miss out on the beauty that surrounds us here."

His arm came around her, and he stroked her hair back out of her face. "He has a point. This place is incredible. I always thought about spending a week at one of the cabins on the lake here. Do you have any idea how happy that would make me?"

"Sounds great, but not for a honeymoon. I don't need to be surrounded by family as I'm getting used to being intimate with my new husband."

"Yeah, your brothers would be checking on you too frequently. I might have to kill them and throw their bodies in the lake." He shook his head. "I've obviously been hanging out with you Westons too much lately. I never threaten to kill people! I'm the law around here, you know."

Kelsi grinned, leaning against him. "You are, and we're all grateful for that fact." She took a deep breath. "Do you think we're making a mistake getting married so quickly? I'm really kind of being cowardly by planning it this way…"

"No, I don't. I think it's the perfect solution. That way you're not hurting anyone's feelings, and I get to have you all to myself that much sooner. It works very well for me!"

She laughed softly. "I think you're thinking about your own interests and not anyone else's."

"Well, yours and mine. I'm helping you out of a bind, if you'll remember!"

"And that's the real reason you're marrying me so fast, right?"

He grinned, leaning down to kiss her softly. "What do you think?"

They sat and talked about their future, ate a bit, and then talked some more. It was just getting dark when they dropped off the four-wheelers at the shed.

"Where'd you park?" he asked.

"At the house. I can walk back."

He shook his head. "I'm not letting you walk that far by yourself after dark."

"It's only a ten-minute walk!" she protested. "I've lived here my whole life. I don't remember the last time there was a violent crime in this part of Idaho."

"Then it's time for one, so you should be extra careful…and don't forget poor George! People are killed accidentally!" He wasn't letting her get off that easily. She was going to be safe if it killed him.

Kelsi shook her head at him, but didn't complain when he wrapped an arm around her shoulders and walked with her toward the house. It was odd to think that she wouldn't live there much longer. It had been her home since the day she'd come home from the hospital.

After a quick kiss at the door, Kelsi went into the house

alone. She was surprised to find Dani waiting up for her. "What's going on?" she asked.

"Oh, Mom's being a pain. She wants me to set up this date between you and Bobby on the night he arrives, and I'm not doing it. You'll already be married by then!"

Kelsi wrinkled her nose. "Did you tell Mom the sheriff and I are getting serious? You can do that without revealing wedding plans."

Dani sighed. "I didn't even think about it."

Kelsi frowned, opening her door and noting that her sister followed her in. "Will you do a spa day with me on Saturday?" she asked softly. "I know you hate spa days, but I want my sister with me. And Jess, of course. Do you think Jess would do it?"

Dani shrugged. "I have no idea, but I think it would be fun for the three of us to do together," she said, her face looking like she'd just swallowed an extra-sour lemon.

"You're a good sister, you know that?"

Dani wrinkled her nose. "Are we going to just play in the afternoon? If not, I'm going to have to beg Shane to play short-order sheriff again. I hear his deputies always come in so they can complain about his cooking when he takes over for me."

Kelsi laughed. "They do. I think it's hilarious."

"You're going to have to start taking his side on everything once you marry, you know."

"Why?" Kelsi asked.

"Because it's the Weston way."

"But I'm going to be a Clapper, not a Weston."

"That's unfortunate. You will still have Weston genes, though, so you'll have to continue to behave like one of us. Every day for the rest of your life." Dani smiled, getting to her feet. "We need to have a bachelorette party for you on Friday night. Maybe some slasher movies? Popcorn? Pie?"

"How do you know me so well?" Kelsi asked with a wink.

"Because you've always been my built-in best friend." Dani hugged her. "Look at me, getting all maudlin. Don't expect this to happen again!"

Kelsi smiled. "I won't. I know that you're above the feelings we lesser mortals have. You're tougher than that."

"So true. Don't tell the others I was nice to you. They might start expecting it, and it's just not going to happen." Dani started to close the door behind her.

"Hey, Dani?"

"Yeah?"

"I love you."

"Whatever. Me too, I guess." Dani grinned at her twin and closed the door behind her.

Kelsi changed into her pajamas, thinking about how special her sister was to her. They may not always appear to be close or get along, and Dani may grumble a lot more than most people, but Kelsi couldn't think of anyone she'd rather have at her side for her wedding. Maybe she could get her to blond her hair for it, so they could actually look like twins again.

She shook her head, dismissing the idea before she even proposed it to her sister. She enjoyed having her own identity too much for her to be willing to look that much like her sister again.

After brushing her teeth, Kelsi climbed into bed and folded her hands behind her head, staring up at the ceiling. Her life was about to change in a way she'd never expected. She just hoped she was doing the right thing.

* * *

Shane stayed up late making room in his closet for Kelsi's

clothes and trying to get everything situated. He hoped she didn't have as much stuff as he did, because there wasn't much room left in his junk room.

When he finally got into bed, he laid with his eyes open for a long time, thinking of her. He hoped that marrying immediately was the right thing for her, like it was for him. He didn't know if he'd have been able to stand a long engagement anyway. After four years of waiting, it already felt like it had been forever.

Soon they'd be married and he'd be the happiest man on earth. He only wished he could be just as sure of Kelsi's happiness.

Chapter Eight

By Friday night, Kelsi realized she was very nervous about marrying the sheriff, and she couldn't figure out why. He was a good man, one who loved her beyond her wildest expectations. So why did the idea of the wedding make her so nervous?

When she met up with her sister and cousin in Jess's cabin—one that was usually reserved for guests, but she'd claimed as her own when she'd started veterinary school— she felt her stomach rumbling with nerves.

Jess opened the door to welcome her, and she was surprised to see that Dani was already there. The whole house smelled of popcorn and pie, and Kelsi felt tears well up in her eyes. They'd done exactly what she wanted.

"You guys are the best sisters a girl could ever ask for."

Jess smiled. "I'm glad you wanted to do this. I needed a night off from studying to be with my favorite cousins."

"What movie are we watching?" Kelsi asked, excited.

Dani and Jess exchanged looks. "We didn't want to have to watch a slasher movie tonight." Dani looked almost nervous when she told her.

Kelsi frowned. "So what are we watching? Not a rom com. Tell me you guys don't expect me to sit here and put up with watching a stupid romantic comedy!"

Dani sighed. "Jess wanted to watch *Notting Hill*, but I didn't think you'd like that."

"No! Please tell me you nixed that idea!"

"I did! I figured if we weren't going to watch a slasher, we couldn't watch a rom com, so we compromised." She pulled a superhero movie from behind her back.

Kelsi shrugged. "Better than a rom com I guess."

"I made popcorn, and I got you some jalapeno-cheddar seasoning for your bowl!" Jess said with a grin.

"Sometimes I think no one knows me at all, and then I realize you guys couldn't love me as much as you do if you didn't know me." Kelsi sighed contentedly, thrilled about the seasoning. It was such a small thing, but it made her realize her cousin really had thought of her.

She sat down on one end of the couch, knowing her sister and cousin would want to share a bowl of popcorn. She sprinkled a generous amount of seasoning on her own bowl and waited while Dani put the movie in. "Thanks for bachelorette-partying with me, girls."

Dani shrugged. "I can put up with spending time with you two, as long as you're not expecting me to go to some strip club and stick dollar bills on mostly naked men."

Kelsi wrinkled her nose. "I can think of many things I'd rather do!"

Halfway through the movie they paused it to move on to the pie portion of the evening. "Warm huckleberry pie!" Kelsi said, accepting the plate from Jess. "Did you get it from the restaurant?"

"Well, I sure didn't have time to bake it!" Jess retorted, handing Dani a piece of pie, before going back for her own.

Kelsi didn't care who made it, but the restaurant had the best huckleberry pie recipe in the whole state of Idaho, so she smiled as she sank her fork into it. "Do you know Shane had never had huckleberry pie until our first date? Who let him live in Idaho without trying huckleberry pie first? It should be a criminal offense." She grinned. "I think he should have to arrest himself and spend a couple of days in jail."

Dani shook her head. "Without you? You want to spend your wedding night alone?"

"Maybe not right now. I'll suggest it after our first real fight."

"Looking forward to the first fight?" Dani asked.

"Nope. But I know it's inevitable. I fight with everyone I love. I'm good at it." Kelsi knew she was quirky and not always the easiest person in the world to get along with. It was part of her charm.

Jess laughed and moved around the coffee table to sit down with her own pie. "I hope he makes you as happy as you deserve to be."

Kelsi looked at her cousin with her eyebrows drawn together. "I'm not sure if that's a good wish or a bad one."

"Take it how you will!"

* * *

Kelsi met Dani at the ranch's spa the following morning. Jess had claimed to be too busy with schoolwork to take enough time off to be there for the bachelorette party, spa day, *and* the wedding. She had chosen the two most important, and begged off the third.

"Are you excited for this?" Kelsi asked Dani.

Dani sighed. "I'm doing it, aren't I?" The look on her face left Kelsi with no doubt she was dreading every minute of the experience.

Kelsi threaded her arm through her sister's. "I guess for now that'll have to be enough!" Together they walked to the front desk and introduced themselves. The spa was relatively new, and neither had been there yet. "We're Kelsi and Dani Weston. We have appointments."

The girl at the desk looked up, her eyes wide. "Yes, of course. I'm Angela Myers. You can call me Angie. I'm the manager here."

Kelsi smiled, reaching out a hand to shake the other woman's. "It's nice to meet you! We want the works."

"I have you scheduled for massages, waxing, mani-pedis, and then facials. Am I missing anything?" Angie asked, obviously nervous.

"That sounds about right. There's a lunch in there too, right?"

"Yes, Miss Weston. I've ordered the soup and sandwiches you wanted to be brought in from the café here on property."

Kelsi grinned. "I guess we know who's making our lunch then."

Angie gave them a blank smile. Obviously they'd done a better job than Kelsi realized keeping the wedding quiet. Earlier, Kelsi had gone in to see how the wedding cake preparations were coming along at the restaurant before leaving the house, and she was pleased. It was all falling into place.

She and Shane had gone for their marriage license the previous day, and he'd promised to be on time, wearing his Sunday best.

Dani and Kelsi were led to a small waiting room and given glasses of water with some kind of pieces of fruit floating in them. Dani hated water with floating stuff, but she didn't complain.

"The only service you won't be together for is your massage. You'll have facials at the same time in the same room, and your mani-pedis will be together as well. The waxing will be done in the same room as your massages, so I guess that will be apart too." Angie frowned. "Do you have any questions for me?"

Kelsi thought hard to come up with a question. "If you were a small animal, what kind of animal would you be?"

Angie's eyes widened and she looked at Dani as if to find out if Kelsi really needed an answer.

Dani shook her head. "Ignore my sister. She lost her grip on reality a long time ago."

Angie hurried out of the room, obviously afraid Kelsi was going to ask her something else.

Kelsi frowned at Dani. "I really wanted to know! She reminded me of one of Jaclyn's frightened bunny rabbits. Or maybe a squirrel. I could see her as a squirrel."

"Hey, Kelsi?"

"Yeah, Dani?"

"You're scary sometimes."

Kelsi shrugged. "I don't mean to be. Sometimes I'm just curious, so I ask the questions I'm curious about."

"Sometimes it might be better if you held your questions in."

"But what if I explode from wonderingness?"

Dani sighed. "You won't explode. You'll be just fine." She looked up as someone came into the room.

"I'm looking for Miss Weston," the woman said softly.

"We're both Miss Weston. Which one?" Kelsi asked.

"Kelsi," the woman said. She was obviously nervous as well.

"I'm Kelsi Weston. Are you going to massage me until I don't remember my name?"

The girl laughed softly. "Yes, I will do my very best. I'm Maddie, by the way."

Kelsi stood up to follow her. "This is my first massage. You'll have to tell me how it all works."

She waved to her sister as she followed Maddie out of the room and into a small room with a table in the middle. "I need you to get undressed as much as you're comfortable undressing. You can keep your panties on if you feel more comfortable that way, but the bra definitely needs to go. Then get face down on the table with your head in the hole. Cover up with the sheet. I'll give you five minutes to get undressed."

Kelsi stripped down, leaving her panties on, because it felt too awkward otherwise. She laid face down on the table and waited. It seemed like forever before Maddie stepped back into the room.

"Are you comfortable?" Maddie asked.

Kelsi lifted her face from the hole. "I guess so. Why is my face in a hole?"

Maddie chuckled softly, coating her hands in oil. "To make it so you can breathe. I'm going to start with your back and work my way to your legs. Let me know if the pressure is too soft or too hard."

Kelsi felt weird having someone touch her so intimately without knowing anything about her. "Tell me about you."

"Well, let's see. I'm from Iowa, and I went to massage school there. I wanted to see more of the world, so I spent a year doing massage on cruise ships, but that didn't feel right for me. So I spent a month with my parents, and I saw an ad for a new spa opening at a dude ranch in Idaho. Sounded like the life for me, so I came here. I've been here since the spa opened, so about a month, I guess."

"What do you think of Idaho?"

"It's so beautiful! I would love to stay here forever. This is your family's ranch, isn't it?"

Kelsi and Maddie chatted through the ninety-minute massage. When she was done, Maddie used a towel to dry off Kelsi's legs. "Your wax is next, but I don't torture people like that. I bring pleasure not pain."

Kelsi sighed. "I've never had a wax either. Is it bad?"

"What all are you getting done?"

"Eyebrows, underarms, and legs."

Maddie frowned. "Legs will be the worst. Just don't kick Karen. She's my friend!"

"I'll do my best. It doesn't sound pleasant."

"It's not. I'd rather shave any day." Maddie left, and Kelsi lay staring at the ceiling, worried about the pain that was coming. Did she have to go through with this?

Fifteen minutes later, Kelsi met Dani in the waiting room, where they had water and soup waiting for them. "I don't think I like being waxed," Kelsi said, rubbing one of her legs. She was wearing the robe Maddie had left for her, but she wasn't particularly feeling great.

Dani frowned. "It wasn't something I see myself doing regularly either. What's wrong with a good old-fashioned razor in the summers, when a razor is needed? I don't exactly keep my leg hair fashionably shaved for summer."

"Who does?" Kelsi asked. "My motto is, if it's not braidable through your jeans, there's no need to mess with it in the winter."

"Are you still going to do that when you're married?"

"We're going to have to see how I feel about leg hair when winter comes…and if it bothers Shane. Who knows?"

By the time they'd been pampered all day, Kelsi felt like a noodle that had been cooked a little too long. As they walked home from the spa, she sighed. "That was nice. Now I want to sleep for a week or two."

"You seeing the sheriff tonight?" Dani asked.

Kelsi shrugged. "He didn't say anything, so I don't know."

When they got to the house, they had their answer. Shane was sitting on the back porch waiting for her. He stood up and walked over, nodding at Dani. "Did you ladies have fun?"

Dani shrugged. "It didn't kill me." Without another word she walked into the house, leaving Shane staring at the closed door.

"Why does your sister hate me?" he asked, shaking his head.

"She doesn't! She thinks you're good for me. She treats everyone that way." She stood on tiptoe and kissed him softly. "What are you doing here?"

"I thought you might want to go into town for dinner or something." He looked down at his hands. "Really? I needed to see you. I had this dream you were backing out, and I needed to make sure you were going through with the wedding."

She laughed softly. "Of course, I'm going through with it. Can you see me being the happy wife of Bobby Blakely?"

"I don't want to imagine you being the wife of anyone else, happy or not." He brushed his lips across hers. "Do you want to do dinner?"

Kelsi thought about everything she needed to do that night and frowned. "How 'bout we get the restaurant to make us a pizza to share, and you can help me pack up my room."

"Oh, I wasn't thinking about you having to pack tonight."

She shrugged. "I don't have a ton left to do, but it's enough that I don't want to put it off. If I'm not here, we can be renting my room out and making money on it."

He followed her down a hall to an employees only door and watched as she went through it. "Come on. You're with me!" She grabbed his hand and pulled him into the kitchen with her.

She went to the chef, Samuel, who looked at her with a sigh. "You always want something."

"Sam, you know I'm your favorite. I just need one little favor…"

"You fought with your brother in my restaurant again. I told you to stop that nonsense!"

"He was being a pain. You know how Will gets, spending every waking moment trying to find new ways to torment me." She put her hand on his arm. "It's a little favor…"

"What do you want? You know I'll do anything for you!" Sam had been the chef at the restaurant since Kelsi was six, and she'd spent a lot of time cajoling him into making her things she shouldn't have.

"We want a pizza."

"A *pizza*? I was trained in one of the finest culinary institutions in this country, and you want me to make you a *pizza*?"

She smiled sweetly. "A kitchen sink pizza! Add everything you can find!"

Sam sighed. "You want chicken again?"

"Of course!"

"I refuse to add fish this time. That was disgusting to even look at."

"When you grill the chicken, add some of my Cajun seasoning."

"Fine. You go. I'll have it brought to your room." Sam looked at Shane. "You gonna be in her room?"

"I was going to help her with something there."

"You'll leave the door cracked. She's like a daughter to me."

Kelsi stood on tiptoe and kissed Sam's cheek. "Thanks, Sam!"

She grabbed Shane's hand and tugged him out of the kitchen and toward her bedroom. "He thinks we're doing something wrong," Shane said, frowning at her as soon as they were in her room. "You should have told him we're getting married tomorrow."

"I couldn't. He has my mother on speed dial." She walked to a bookshelf and handed him a box. "All the books go in the box. I have my Kindle out, so I can still read before bed."

Shane nodded, getting right to work. He noted the titles as he packed them away. All she seemed to have were Stephen King, Edgar Allen Poe, and H. P. Lovecraft. "Don't you read anything but horror?" he called.

She came out of her closet with her arms full of shoes. "Of course not. Well, I did when I was in school, but thankfully that nonsense is over. Now I read for pleasure, and to me, that means horror."

"Do you ever get scared when you read and watch so much horror?"

She piled the shoes into the bottom of a box, slowly adding other things. "Sure. That's part of the fun." She shrugged. "As long as my feet are under the covers, the monsters can't get me."

He sighed. "Am I going to have to look for monsters under the bed?"

She grinned at him. "Would you if I asked?"

He caught her hand and pulled her down onto his lap,

kissing her softly. "I have a feeling I'd do anything you asked of me."

"Deciding to marry you is the smartest thing I've ever done." She sighed, resting her cheek against his shoulder.

"You only say that because the fairies told you to marry me."

"Can I tell you a secret?"

He nodded, his eyes wary. "I guess."

"I think the gnomes and leprechauns are a whole lot more trustworthy than the fairies."

"Sometimes I'm not sure whether I should be afraid, or just love you."

She sighed, kissing him. "I think loving me is always the answer."

There was the sound of a loud throat clearing coming from her doorway. "Thanks, Sam." She jumped up and took the tray from him, which contained the pizza and two plates.

"Why are you packing?" he asked. "You're not moving in with the sheriff. Over my dead body!"

Kelsi sighed. "You know the big wedding the kitchen is getting ready to cater tomorrow?"

Sam nodded. "Yes?"

"That's *our* wedding. We're not telling people, because Mom wants me to marry a boy I knew in elementary school who chased me around with reptiles."

Sam frowned. "So you want me to keep this a secret from your mother?" The idea seemed to pain him.

"Please? Just for twenty-four hours. Jaclyn knows, and she approves."

Sam rolled his eyes. "Did the fairies tell her that you two should marry?"

Kelsi nodded emphatically. "They did!"

"Please tell me that's not the only reason you're

marrying him." Sam looked from Kelsi to Shane. "I want you to be happy, kiddo."

Kelsi smiled. "I don't think I could ever find a man who loves me more than Shane does. Being married to him will make me happy," she said. And it was true. But would being married to her make *him* happy?

Sam shrugged. "I won't say anything." He looked at Shane. "You treat her right."

Shane got to his feet, holding his hand out to shake the chef's. "She's really special to me. I'm not going to hurt her in any way."

"See that you don't." Sam left the room, leaving the tray on her bed. Shane noticed he left the door more than a little ajar.

"He's worried about you."

"Sam's always been there for me, and I've been special to him. He was the one who held me the day my grandma died. Mom and Dad were busy with Granddad and making the funeral arrangements. Sam had time for me."

Shane nodded. "I just wish you didn't have the whole world watching us to make sure I didn't hurt you. It's... hard on me sometimes."

"I can't change the people who love me, and I wouldn't. It feels good to have people care so much."

"I understand." He put pizza on two plates and handed one to her, looking at the pizza curiously. "A kitchen sink pizza?"

"Oh yeah. He throws on just about everything. I love these!"

Shane took a bite, not as excited about all the toppings as she was, but it wasn't terrible. "I can choke this down."

"Soon, you won't even need me to make you spiced-down enchiladas!"

"Don't count on that. I want to still have taste buds… not burn them off."

She grinned, taking a huge bite of her pizza. He was coming around, and she was so glad.

* * *

Kelsi had a regular hairdresser in town, and she'd invited her out for the day, promising to pay her triple, and telling her to bring her supplies. Sheila Smyre had been her hairdresser since she was a little girl, and she came grumbling.

Once she arrived, Kelsi told her about the secret wedding, and Sheila squealed with excitement. "I'm doing your hair *and* make-up!"

Kelsi grinned. "I knew I could count on you!" She'd just finished lunch and was ready to get the ball rolling. Getting ready for a wedding was hard work. She sat in her robe, in a chair in her room, and let Sheila do whatever she wanted. She knew the older woman would make her look as good as she possibly could. Why, Sheila was practically a miracle worker!

Dani knocked on her door just as Sheila was finishing up. "Kelsi, I need a trim before the wedding. My hair is out of control again…" She trailed off when she saw the hairdresser in her sister's room. "I'll come back." Dani had once gone to Sheila for her own haircuts, and there was true fear on her face when Dani spotted her.

Sheila grabbed Dani's wrist. "You will not! Today is your sister's wedding day, and you're going to look your best if it means I have to sit on you to fix your hair. Kelsi knows nothing about hair!" Sheila threaded her fingers through Dani's hair, groaning loudly. "Do you have any idea what a mess she's made of this?"

Dani shrugged. "It doesn't bother me."

"I'll fix it decently today, and give you a trim. One that will flatter you and not look like someone took a butcher knife to your head."

"It's not that bad," Dani protested.

Sheila stopped her with a look, turning back to Kelsi. "You go and get your dress on now, and I'll deal with your sister." She shook her head at Dani. "Short is fine. Butchered is not. It will be fixed today."

Kelsi bit her lip at the look on her twin's face as she hurried from the room, taking her dress into Dani's to get ready. She couldn't quite get the buttons done up herself, so when she was finished, she left the back of the dress gaping and stood outside her bedroom door, listening for yells. When she heard nothing, she stepped into her room.

What she saw shocked her. Dani was sitting meekly while Sheila worked her magic. Kelsi sometimes forgot that they could be identical, because they'd worked so hard not to be. Dani looked pretty for a change, sitting there with her short hair styled into something that looked decent.

"You look beautiful, Dani."

Dani made a face. "I look all made-up."

"Not yet," Sheila answered. "But you will before I'm done with you! Go and get dressed, and I'll do your make-up after I finish Kelsi's." Just before Dani left, she stopped her. "If you ever let your sister touch your hair with scissors again, you will feel my wrath."

Dani nodded and hurried away.

As soon as she was gone, Kelsi burst out laughing. "I think you scared her, Sheila!"

"I hope I did! And *you*! You stop whacking her hair off every time she asks!"

"If I don't do it, she will. And she does an even worse job than I do! What am I supposed to do?"

"Call me out here. For that girl, I will make house

calls!" Sheila waved at the chair Dani had just vacated. "Sit!"

"Would you do my dress up first?" Kelsi asked, turning her back to the other woman.

Sheila immediately complied. "This dress is beautiful. Old."

"It was Grandma Kelsey's. I always knew I'd wear it someday." Kelsi wondered if her sister would wear it when she married.

"It suits you!"

When she was finished with the buttons, Kelsi sat down and waited patiently while Sheila did her make-up. Dani slipped into the room during the process, wearing the ice blue dress Kelsi had chosen for her to borrow. "You look wonderful. Your eyes look so amazing in that color."

Dani sat on the edge of the bed, obviously feeling uncomfortable in the pretty dress. "You mean *our* eyes. The ones that are identical. I look like *you* with short hair today."

Kelsi frowned. "It's not a bad thing for us to look alike every once in a while. Just not every day. Trust me, today, everyone will know I'm me, because I'm dressed in the wedding dress." She grinned. "Besides, I'll be the one in the bridal mouse ears!" She nodded to the box sitting on her otherwise empty nightstand.

Dani grinned. "I suppose you're right. I just hate it when everyone confuses us." She shook her head. "I can't believe you're actually wearing those things to get married in. You'll look ridiculous."

"When was the last time anyone confused us?" Kelsi asked with surprise. It had been years as far as she knew. "I don't care if I look ridiculous. I'll be me."

Dani shrugged. "I don't even remember."

"I think we're safe from confusing people now."

There was a knock on the door, and Dani called for whoever it was to come in.

Will stood there for a moment, his eyes wide. "You both look beautiful."

Dani wrinkled her nose at the compliment, and Kelsi grinned. "You mean *I* look beautiful, and Dani looks like a girl for a change."

Will shrugged. "If you say so." He looked between his sisters. "How much longer? Shane is starting to freak out."

Kelsi looked at the clock on her wall. "Tell Shane to get a grip. Wedding isn't supposed to start for another thirty minutes. I'm almost ready, and Dani will be ready in ten minutes. We got this." Wasn't it the bride who was supposed to get nervous before the wedding?

Will sighed. "I'll tell him, but he seems really antsy. I'm afraid he's going to start shooting or something."

Kelsi waved her brother away. Surely Shane wasn't as nervous as her brother said. He wasn't the type to freak out so easily. Besides, he would just have to arrest himself if he started causing problems, and she knew he didn't want to do that.

Chapter Nine

SHANE PACED BACK and forth in front of the little arch that had been placed on the lawn behind the main ranch house. Judging by all the fairies and leprechauns placed at strategic places around the arch, and the two plaster bunnies on the ground beside it, he could guess who was responsible. He hoped the gnomes weren't offended.

Oh, God! Did I seriously just think I hoped the gnomes weren't offended? I'm losing my mind. She's taking my mind down this crazy path, and it's going to be long gone within a week. Bigfoot will be eating it with a knife, a fork, and a good red wine!

Kelsi's brother, Will, wearing his best man suit and a pair of cowboy boots, walked over to him. "She said to stop being nervous, and they'll both be ready within ten minutes or so."

"Nervous? I'm not nervous!" Shane didn't want anyone to think he was nervous. What if they lost respect for him?

Will looked pointedly at the shredded carnation that had been in his lapel not fifteen minutes before. "You sure about that?"

"Is there another one of these?" Shane asked in a

panic, now nervous Kelsi would be angry that he'd shredded the flower he was supposed to wear. "She's going to kill me!" He needed everything to be perfect for his bride on her wedding day, and she'd chosen the carnations, so he would wear a carnation.

Will laughed. "Let me tell you something about Kelsi —" He waited until Shane was looking at him before he continued. "Kelsi is the most even-tempered of all six of us. She believes in forgiveness and love. She doesn't realize it yet, but she's actually the most romantic of our family, and she's always so happy to watch people fall in love. I think she watches the slasher movies so that people don't see her cry with joy when good things happen in real movies."

Shane tilted his head to one side, considering. "I guess that kind of makes sense from what I've seen." It opened up a new side to his sweet bride too.

"Trust me, there's a very soft side to my sister. You've made a good choice. And she has to. I've never seen a couple who is so right for each other." Will unpinned his ice blue carnation and pinned it on the sheriff's lapel. "There. You look perfect. I'll go steal Wyatt's flower. He won't care, and he doesn't have to stand up."

Shane took a deep breath. "Thanks for the pep talk, man."

"No problem. But I bet the girls are about ready, so let me get that flower so I can be best man." Will grinned. "I know you only chose me because Kelsi told you to, but you *did* get the best man."

Shane laughed as he watched the older man walk off, shaking his head. What was it about those Westons that made them so competitive? He was almost surprised none of them had taken up an Olympic sport. It just seemed like something they would do in their family. Of course, with as devoted as they were to the family business, maybe it made sense. Training for the Olympics would take up a lot more time than any of them had available.

Five minutes later, he was standing beside Will in front of the arch when lively music began to play. He and Kelsi hadn't talked about music, so he was surprised. Why wasn't she walking to the *Wedding March* like a normal person? Only Kelsi would walk down the aisle at her wedding to the *William Tell Overture*.

First he saw Dani, seeming to walk at a sedate pace befitting a bridesmaid, but then getting into the spirit of the music and practically galloping to the arch. She gave him a very confused look as she took her spot, as if she had no idea how she'd gotten there so quickly.

Then he turned his attention to watching as his bride left the house and headed his way. She wasn't doing anything sedately, because it wasn't in her nature. Instead she bumped hips with the man escorting her and even gave a quick twirl on her way to him. He grinned, trying to figure out how he'd gotten so lucky as to find a woman like her to be his bride.

He squinted, trying to see whose arm she held. He knew it couldn't be her father, and all her brothers were present and accounted for. And then he knew. Sam. The chef in her family's restaurant was walking her down the aisle. Maybe that was part of her reasoning for not wanting her mother there. She'd wanted to do things her own way, and no mother in her right mind would allow her daughter to walk down the aisle to the *William Tell Overture* on one of the family employee's arms. *Only Kelsi.*

When she reached him, it was all he could do not to reach out and move a strand of hair that was hanging a bit oddly from her mouse ears. It was probably meant to be that way, and he'd ruin her whole look if he tried to change it, so he didn't, taking her hand only when the pastor told him to.

The ceremony was short, but it did the job. When he was told he could kiss his bride, the grin he gave her was part relief, but a whole lot of pride. Putting his hands on her waist, he drew her close to him, pressing his lips to hers.

He lifted his head too quickly to Kelsi's way of thinking, so she wrapped her arms around his neck, pulling his head down for one more kiss. Shane heard the laughter of the few people she'd invited, but he didn't care. It was obvious she wanted to kiss him, so who could complain?

After the pastor had introduced them to the crowd as Mr. and Mrs. Shane Clapper, they turned to face their audience. There were less than twenty people there, but Kelsi saw almost everyone she loved—and absolutely everyone she had wanted to be there. She was overwhelmed as she saw so many people who would die for her, and she had no doubt that every single one of them would.

She took Shane's hand and dragged him over to Jaclyn Hardy. "Thank you for the arch, Jaclyn. It's perfect!"

"The fairies suggested it. I just did as they asked."

"Well, I'm proud to have been married under it." Kelsi hugged the older woman tightly. "You're staying for food, right? We had the restaurant make all of their specialties." She hadn't seen Jaclyn this far from her home in years. Usually she put in orders for whatever she needed, so she was glad the woman was there. Since her Grandma Kelsey had died, Jaclyn had become more and more of a recluse, preferring the company of her fairies and bunnies to the real world.

Jaclyn nodded. "I wouldn't miss this for the whole world."

"You sit down and I'll fix you a plate." Kelsi took the older woman's arm to walk her to a table.

"No, you go fix your own plate. I told you before. I'm not sick, just old. The more I do for myself, the more I'll be able to do for myself. You're not running me off anytime soon!"

"Yes, ma'am," Kelsi answered, not bothered by her words. "You take care of yourself and I'll take care of myself."

"Why would you take care of yourself when you have that sexy man to take care of you?" Jaclyn asked.

Shane blushed. Was a woman old enough to be his grandmother allowed to call him sexy? He didn't know, but he was certainly a bit intimidated by it.

Kelsi wandered through the crowd gathered for her wedding, finding her brother Wade and hugging him. "I know it worried you to not tell Mom, but thank you for respecting my wishes."

Wade closed his eyes as he held her. "You sure do make my life difficult sometimes, Kelsi, but you're not too bad on the eyes. You have *something* going for you."

"Uh-huh." Kelsi grinned over at Shane. "Let's eat! And then we need to cut the cake, but real food first."

"How are you going to be happy with the food? You're not carrying your purse…"

She looked both ways to make sure no one was watching before pulling a tiny can of Cajun seasoning from her cleavage. "I've got it covered."

Shane laughed, grabbing her and kissing her. "Life with you is never going to be boring, is it?" Was there any other woman in the world who would carry Cajun seasoning in her cleavage at her wedding? He knew his sweet bride was a one of a kind.

"I sure hope not…"

Two hours later, they were headed to his place, both of their trucks filled to the max with her things. It didn't seem like she had a lot until she started pulling the boxes out from under her bed.

They met in the driveway of his house, and he sighed loudly, looking at the trucks. "This is going to be a lot of work. I'm not sure I want to do all this on my wedding day."

"You don't have to!" Didn't he have any idea of the family he'd married into?

He frowned. "I guess I *could* leave it 'til tomorrow, but we only have one day off together before going back to work."

"That's not what I mean." She jerked her thumb toward the street.

What he saw was something beyond anything he'd dreamed of. All of her brothers, her sister, and her cousin were there, already dressed in casual clothes. One after the other, they carried boxes and armfuls of clothes into the house.

Twenty minutes later, there were many thank-yous and hugs as everyone left as quickly as they'd come.

"That was unexpected…" he said, looking at her.

"Now you know why I want twelve kids. Free labor at its finest!"

He took her hand and led her to the door, scooping her into his arms and carrying her over the threshold, before setting her on her feet in the living room. "I still can't believe you wore red cowboy boots with your wedding dress!" He shook his head. "When you pulled up your skirt for that line dance, I almost fell over!"

"I *told* you I was going to. They look good, don't they?" She looked down at one of her boots before looking at him with a grin. "I may be strange, but I've always been this way. You chose me!"

He nodded, pulling her to him for a kiss. "And I'd do it again every day for the rest of my life."

She sighed, resting her head on his shoulder. She wished she could say the same. She wanted to tell him she loved him, because he deserved the words, but he didn't deserve to be lied to. No, she'd wait until she was ready.

* * *

When Kelsi got to work early Saturday morning, she popped her head into the kitchen, expecting to see her sister getting ready to start her day. Instead, she saw Dani standing with a man she'd never seen before. He was handsome, but there was something that just seemed...*off.*

"Hi, I'm Kelsi," she said.

The man turned to her and grinned, and then she knew.

"Bobby Blakely." In her newly-wedded bliss—and being married to Shane could only be described as bliss—she'd forgotten all about Bobby coming. It should have been more awkward, but she didn't mind. A romance between the two of them could only have happened in her mother's mind.

He shook his head. "Just Bob now. I outgrew Bobby in the sixth grade."

"Welcome home," Kelsi said softly, refusing to be impolite, even though she wanted to yell at him to get out of her café.

"Thanks. And thanks for getting married before I got here. Do you realize your mother came to see me every day for a week, telling me that I needed to marry *you*, and *only* you? She told me Dani is all wrong for me, but you would be my perfect wife." He shuddered. "I was afraid she was saying all the same things to you!"

"She was, until I told her Monday morning that I'd gotten married."

"You married the sheriff, right?" Bob grinned, waiting for her nod before continuing. "Do you have any idea how relieved that makes me? Even if I was madly in love with you, I'm not stupid enough to take on a man who carries a gun for his job!"

"Glad to hear it!" Kelsi couldn't believe how relieved she felt. "I'm glad you're going to be cooking for us. Mom says you're amazing!" He wasn't going to be terrible to work with after all. She wanted to spread her arms and spin in circles she was so excited.

He nodded. "I am. Do you have a problem if I play with the daily specials? Change things up a bit?"

Kelsi shrugged. "I'm perfectly content with that. Just don't go too wild. Maybe make sure there's always one day per week where you fix one of Grandma Kelsey's special recipes."

"I'll do my best."

"Welcome to the team. If you have any questions, feel free to ask me." Kelsi shifted her attention to her twin. "What are you still doing here? Go back to your ordering and other boring paperwork. You're not needed!"

Dani flashed a rare grin. "I'm out of here. See you for supper tomorrow night. Whose turn is it anyway?"

"Will's." When it was Will's turn, the same thing always happened. He went into town and bought pizzas for everyone.

"Pizza? Tell him I don't want one of your nasty every-thing pizzas. Something normal for me!"

Kelsi made a face. "*You* tell him! He's *your* brother too!"

"Yeah, but I just now got a reprieve and don't have to

talk to anyone until dinner tomorrow night. I'll be in my own private version of paradise!"

"And you've helped me a lot. So yeah, I'll call him. Whatever." Kelsi walked into the dining area and sat down, quickly tapping her brother's number. "Will, Dani says only normal pizza for her."

Will groaned. "Is it my turn *again?*"

"Every seventh week, Will. Mark it on your calendar." She hung up before he could complain more, taking a few moments for herself to sit with her thoughts. She wasn't nearly as disgusted with Bob as she'd expected to be. She had seen no turtles, lizards, or snakes on his person, and she'd looked! Maybe he'd grown up just like the rest of them. Wouldn't that be something after all the worrying she'd done?

When Shane came in for lunch at eleven, she sat down across from him as always, putting her feet on his lap for him to rub.

He didn't need to ask what she wanted, immediately sliding her shoes off and massaging her feet, knowing they stayed sore with the hours she worked. "How's it going today?"

"Really good! Bob is here, so Dani's finally off in her little hole of an office, and she's content. He's not nearly as bad as I remembered, so I'm happy too."

"Attractive?"

Kelsi shrugged. "How am I supposed to know?"

"You don't know when a man is attractive?" Shane raised an eyebrow at her.

"I only have eyes for my new husband. He's the sheriff around here, you know!"

Shane grinned. "Whether you mean it or not, you sure do know all the right words to say."

Kelsi laughed. "Well, you *did* promise to take me on a

Bigfoot excursion later." No one in her life had ever been willing to hunt Bigfoot with her as often as Shane has. It made her happy.

"Get a lunch to take with us."

She nodded. "I'll pop into the kitchen and ask Bob for one. He's going to start doing boxed lunches for anyone who wants them on Monday. Fifteen bucks for a lunch for two, including two bottles of water. Not a bad deal if you don't want to do for yourself." She sighed. "What you're doing to my feet is positively wicked! Would you stay all day so I can take periodic breaks?"

He laughed. "I have a lot to do today."

"Like what?"

"Someone needs to grocery shop. I figured once I had a wife, *she'd* do that kind of thing, but *no*! She works six days a week." He frowned at her.

"Well, that's a sexist attitude!" She grinned. "Now that I have a real cook, I could probably cut down to five and spend my weekends grocery shopping *with* you!"

Shane nodded. "I would love that! And then I can put every jalapeno pepper you try to buy back into the produce section where it belongs."

She hopped up and leaned down to kiss his cheek, sliding her feet back into her shoes. "What do you want for lunch? Today's soup is gumbo and the special is blackened chicken."

"It's Saturday! What about the steak?"

"New cook. What will you have?"

He grumbled, "You're going to have to start bringing me a menu. I'll take the gumbo and the blackened chicken, but if it's not good, you'll have to bring me something else."

"It's good!" Kelsi spun around to go put his order in.

Bob looked over at Kelsi as she gave Shane's order. "You look like you were just energized."

"My husband is here and he gave me a foot massage. Seeing him helps, and the foot massage puts me in a blissful place."

"Works for me." He quickly put a piece of chicken, already seasoned, into the oven. "I have to meet this fabulous sheriff of yours."

"Oh, sure! Come on!"

Kelsi led Bob out to meet Shane. "Bob, this is my husband, Shane. Shane, this is Bob, of the reptile reputation."

Bob groaned loudly. "I thought you'd forgotten about the reptiles!"

"Never! I will *forgive* you for the reptiles though, *if* you do a good job."

Looking back and forth between them, Shane saw what her mother had seen. They *would* have made a good couple. They had similar high-energy, peppy personalities.

"It's nice to meet you, Bob." His hand reached for Kelsi's to stake his claim. He wondered how long he'd feel insecure when he saw her with another man.

Bob nodded. "Nice to meet you as well. Her mother…"

Shane grinned at that. "I know. She was hearing it too. Welcome to Riston." He was glad the other man made it obvious he had no interest at all.

"I feel like I'm home again." Bob put his hand on her arm. "Back to the kitchen with me. I'll have the gumbo ready in a minute."

"Why am I jealous of a man whose arrival you've been dreading for weeks?"

She leaned down and kissed him, pulling away when

the door opened and a large party of guests of the ranch came in.

"No idea, but you have nothing to be jealous about. I'm going home with you." She glanced over her shoulder. "Back to work with me. I'll see you around three. I've arranged for a four-wheeler."

"Just one?" he asked, surprised she didn't want to race again—and cheat.

She shrugged. "I kind of like your arms around me while I drive it."

He chuckled softly. "That works for me. It does make it so much nicer…"

As she served the guests, her mind was still on Shane. He was uncertain of her for one reason and one reason only. She hadn't told him she loved him yet. She sighed. She'd felt nothing for the other guys she'd dated, but was what she felt for Shane *love*? How did a person know they were in love? Maybe it was time for another visit to Jaclyn. Lately, the older woman seemed to have all the answers.

* * *

After work on Monday, Kelsi decided to go see her fairy-loving friend instead of hurrying straight home. It was her turn to cook supper, and she was thrilled to have a husband who agreed they should take turns, but she'd started a spicy chili in the crockpot before leaving for work that morning.

As she ambled across the expanse of land toward Jaclyn's, she smiled at the flowers that were starting to bloom all around her. It was hard to believe she'd started dating Shane just three weeks ago, when there was still snow on the ground, and now they were married and the world was starting to look like spring. April was one of her favorite months of the year, because of the change in the weather, and now her anniversary would help her remember to celebrate it by smelling every flower along the way.

The last of the ice had melted from the lake when they'd gone down to sit by it and talk the previous evening. Soon it would be time for the tourists to start pouring in. They had a steady stream all year, of course, but the summer was their busiest time. The ranch had so much to offer from trail rides, the RV park, a nine-hole golf course, to a tent campground and even river rafting. The old West town they'd built was also a big draw, providing first aid, an ice cream shop, and even a general store. She couldn't wait to go rafting herself as soon as it was warm enough. It was one of her favorite things to do, probably because her favorite brother was head of it all.

Will was in charge of all aquatics on the ranch, and he was fabulous with guests. Kelsi just wished he was better at managing employees. He was often taken advantage of, because he was just so affable. He managed not only the river and lake activities, but also the pool. Maybe he was spread too thin and needed an assistant? She had no answers, and she was glad she didn't need them. She'd rather leave management of everything to Wade, who handled it so much better than she ever could.

She navigated through the garden creatures at Jaclyn's and knocked on the door. When Jaclyn opened the door, Kelsi smiled. "I need to talk."

"The tea and snickerdoodles are waiting. Come in! Come in!" Jaclyn's eyes lit up when she saw her, *every* time she saw her. Kelsi needed to make more of an effort to see the older woman, reminding her that she wasn't forgotten and still loved by many.

"You knew I was coming." It wasn't a question. Jaclyn always seemed to know when Kelsi would be visiting.

"The fairies don't like me to be surprised after what happened to poor George…" Jaclyn invited her inside by opening the door wider.

Kelsi could see the tea tray was already on the table, one cup full of milk and the other filled with tea. She walked in and took a seat on the couch, reaching for her milk and cookies. She ate a whole cookie in silence, not sure how to bring up her problem.

"Just spit it out. I don't have time to sit here all day waiting for you to figure out what you want to say." Jaclyn took a sip of tea while she waited, impatiently as usual.

"Well…" Kelsi took a deep breath and another sip of her milk. "How do you know when you love someone?" She felt stupid asking, but at least she was asking Jaclyn and not Will or Dani. They'd have both laughed hysterically like she'd lost a little piece of her mind—okay, another huge chunk of her mind. Whatever.

Jaclyn smiled. "It's different for everyone. Tell me this, though. Close your eyes, and picture yourself in ten years. Is he there?"

Kelsi nodded. "Of course!" Where else would he be? He was Shane.

"Twenty years?"

"Yes, and adult children, and that's downright scary!" She shuddered at the thought of making it through the teen years, immediately wondering if she should re-think the number of children she wanted.

"Now, open your eyes for a moment." After Kelsi had complied, Jaclyn asked, "Is there anyone else you would rather be there than him?"

Kelsi shook her head. "No. Not at all."

"Close your eyes again, and let me tell you a story. Once upon a time, about fifty years ago, there was a young woman who thought she had the whole world at her feet.

There was a young man she wasn't quite sure she loved, but she cared for him a great deal, and she sometimes went out with other men as well. One day, her young man—a police officer—stopped by her house on his way to work. He told her he loved her and he wanted her to be his wife."

"Okay…" Kelsi wasn't sure where the story was going, but she was already enthralled. She could see the comparison to her own life.

"She wasn't sure what she wanted to do. She liked her carefree lifestyle, but she cared a great deal for the young man as well. She promised him she'd give him an answer before the end of the day." Jaclyn took a deep breath. "He said he'd come by as soon as he finished work for the day, because he needed her answer. She went about her daily business as a wealthy young lady. She spent the day shopping with some of her friends. She made sure she was home at five, though, because she knew that would be about the right time for her young man to come. She still wasn't sure if she loved him, and she didn't know what she'd say."

Kelsi smiled, picturing the scene. "Did she say yes?"

"She never had the chance. You see, that young man, who had been in love with her for three years, who had asked her to marry him more than once, and always received the answer, 'not yet,' died in the line of duty that day. When she got the news, that's when she knew. She'd always been able to picture her life with him, but when asked to picture her life *without* him, she dropped to her knees with grief. She couldn't imagine growing old without him at her side. She couldn't imagine ever smiling again if he wasn't with her. And *then* she knew she loved him. Then, when it was too late to tell him. When it was too late to have his children."

Kelsi felt tears stream down her cheeks. "I don't like this story."

"Picture your life without him, Kelsi. Can you do that?" Jaclyn asked softly.

Kelsi opened her eyes, shaking her head. "No, I can't. I don't want to have a life without him!" The very idea hurt her. No, she needed Shane beside her every day for the rest of her life.

"Then you have your answer."

Kelsi reached out a hand and squeezed the older woman's. "What was the girl's name?"

"Jaclyn. And she still thinks of her young police officer every day." Jaclyn's eyes focused on the table between them, and Kelsi saw something that she knew had never been there before. It was a picture of a handsome young police officer with a smiling girl clinging to his arm.

"I'm so sorry."

Jaclyn nodded. "Me too. Not that he died, because I believe that was out of my control. I'm sorry I never told him I loved him. That I didn't have those children to raise after he was gone." She shrugged. "My heart was buried with him."

Kelsi grabbed a tissue to blow her nose and wipe away the tears. "Thank you for your story. What was his name?"

"It was Barry." Jaclyn smiled. "His sister's name was Kelsey. She helped me through it."

"You would have been my *aunt*!" Kelsi had no idea her grandmother had lost a brother who was a police officer. She wondered why it had never come up in their long talks together.

"I feel like I am anyway. Don't you?"

Chapter Ten

Kelsi could think of nothing but the talk she'd had with Jaclyn for the rest of the afternoon. She did some laundry and finished cooking supper, her heart broken for the older woman. No wonder she talked to fairies. She hoped one of them had her Barry's voice.

She had the table set and dinner ready to be served at five, knowing Shane would be home just a few minutes later. She put candles in the middle of the table, ready to have a nice romantic evening with the man she loved. She even had a movie picked out that didn't involve blood and guts. She'd gone with an old superman movie instead, knowing he'd rather not see peoples' brains gush out their ears, no matter how much she liked it.

She was curled on the couch, reading one of her favorite books, her mind half on the book and half on what she was going to say to Shane when he came home, when her phone rang.

It wasn't until then she realized he was late. With trepidation she checked the display, frowning as she answered it. "Hi, Mom."

"Hi, Kelsi."

It was the first time her mother had called her since she'd told her about marrying Shane, so she wasn't sure if this was going to be a good call or not.

"Where are you and Dad now?" she asked, acting as if nothing had happened.

There was a pause. "We're in Florida. With all the times we've been to Disneyland, we thought it was time we tried Disney World. It's so big in comparison!"

Kelsi grinned, knowing she'd been forgiven. She'd known she would be, but she didn't know *when*. "Have you been to all the parks yet?"

"Yes! I think Epcot is my favorite by far."

Kelsi sat back and listened to her mother go on and on about the wonders of Disney World, but the longer they talked, the more concerned she became. Shane hadn't been late getting home from work since they'd married, and he was more than an hour late already.

Finally, her mother changed the subject. "So how's married life? Are you and the sheriff getting along?"

Kelsi smiled as she thought of the man she loved, glancing toward the door, hoping she just hadn't heard him come in somehow. "Yeah. He's really a wonderful man, and I'm lucky to have him."

"I'm glad you're happy. Let Wade know the first part of our instructions will be coming this week."

"Wait, the first part? I thought there was *one* test we had to pass." Why did her mother have to make everything so *complicated?*

"Oh, there is. It just comes in multiple parts. I love you."

The phone went dead, and Kelsi stared at it for a moment before walking to the door and peering out the window. Where could he be? She quickly dialed his number, saying a little prayer that he'd answer. She couldn't remember being this frightened in years—and she watched horror movies by the dozens!

Shane answered, sounding tired. "Hey, you."

She breathed again. "Are you all right?" She wanted to yell at him for being late and not calling, but what good would that do? She wanted them to grow closer, not drive a wedge between them.

"There was a kerfuffle in town today…two men were fighting over the last grocery cart, and…I got hurt trying to break them up."

Kelsi bit her lip, unsure of whether to laugh or cry. "*How* hurt?"

"Stitches on my arm. One of them shoved me, and I fell and cut my arm. I'm just now leaving the hospital. I'll be there in thirty or so."

"Do I need to come get you? Can you drive?" Trust Riston to be a place where the sheriff got hurt breaking up a fight over a grocery cart.

"No, I'm fine. Bart drove me, and he waited. He'll bring me home."

"All right. I'll see you soon." She paced back and forth, wondering how deep the cut was for him to have to have stitches. She'd seen her brothers go through all sorts of minor injuries over the years, and she herself had broken an arm skiing when she was younger. Still, she worried.

When she heard a car in the drive, she ran to the door, flinging it open. Bart was there, standing by as if he was sure he needed to help Shane. "Thanks for bringing him home, Deputy Bart!"

"You got it, Mrs. Clapper!"

She started at the sound of her new name. It seemed

strange, because she hadn't used it yet. "Do you need help?" she asked, worried at the size of the bandage on his arm.

"No, I'm fine." He shook his head, a bit pale but otherwise no worse for the wear. "My first work-related injury, and I fell and sliced my arm on a broken jar of jam." The disgust in his voice over the way the injury had happened told her that it wasn't serious.

She bit her lip, struggling not to giggle at the disgruntled sound of his voice. "Come on. I have dinner waiting."

As soon as he was in the house, Bart touched the brim of his hat and left to get in his car.

"Thank you!" Kelsi called.

Bart waved as he pulled out, and Kelsi walked behind Shane, making sure he got to the table. "Are you hungry? I made chili."

He nodded. "Starving actually. Did you make it too hot?" He looked at her warily, nervous about eating food she considered fit for human consumption. He didn't know how she did it.

She shook her head. "I have seasoning to add." She put a bowl in front of him and sat down with her own. She shook both Cajun seasoning and chili powder into her bowl before tasting it, making sure it was seasoned to her taste. "Can you work tomorrow? Should I call and say I need to stay home with you?"

"I can go in. They don't want me to drive 'til the stitches are out, but I can do the paperwork I keep avoiding. I'm sure I have enough to keep me busy for a month. It will teach me to get between two great-grandfathers fighting over a grocery cart." He shook his head, obviously exasperated.

She hid her grin. "Okay, but if you need me, give me a call. I can leave work if I need to."

"Absolutely not." Shane noticed the candles on the table for the first time. "Was there something special going on tonight?" He felt awful that she'd gone to extra trouble, and he hadn't been there to celebrate whatever it was she was excited about.

Kelsi wasn't sure it was a good time to tell him with his injury and all. "Well, we have been married *eight days* now." She said it with so much enthusiasm, he had to laugh.

"A whole eight days? Sounds like reason to celebrate to me."

She grinned at that. "I saw Jaclyn for a little while today."

"The fairies weren't mean to you, were they? Bigfoot and I will go after them if they were. Just give me a few days to heal!" Teasing her about Bigfoot came as naturally as kissing her.

She made a face. "The fairies are never mean to me. They love me. No, I stopped by for a chat. I try to check on her at least once a week, but she would hate it if she knew that." She shook her head. Stubborn and bull-headed didn't begin to describe Jaclyn.

He nodded. "I can see that. She seems very independent."

"She never married."

Shane shrugged. "I assumed as much since she's Miss Hardy and not Mrs. Hardy. Why bring that up now?"

"She told me a story today." Kelsi looked down at the table, wondering how much she should tell him.

"If it was about the fairies, I'm not sure I can handle it!"

She shook her head. "No, it wasn't about the fairies at all. In a way it was about how she met my grandmother, but not really."

"Are you planning to tell me this story? Or will you

make me guess?" Whatever it was she'd talked to Jaclyn about, it was obviously very important to her.

Kelsi sighed. "You don't need to hear the whole thing. You just need to know that she helped me realize I've been really wrong about something."

He frowned, a bite of chili paused in front of his mouth. "About what?"

"I found Bigfoot."

He blinked a few times. "You found *Bigfoot*?" She couldn't be serious.

"No, but I did realize I love you."

He tilted his head to one side, considering her. "Maybe I do need to hear this whole story."

She shrugged. "Probably not. It just made me realize that I've loved you for a while, but never having been in love before, I didn't recognize the signs." She felt stupid admitting it, but it was the truth. Besides, if you couldn't be stupid in front of the man you loved, who could you be stupid in front of?

He reached with his good hand to grip one of hers. "I love you too."

"I know. And that's why I was so excited to be able to tell you." She took a drink of her water. "I'm not sure why it took me so long to realize it, but I promise, I won't forget again." She'd spend the rest of her life loving him, just as Jaclyn had spent the rest of her life loving Barry. Maybe it was silly, but she knew no matter what happened, she'd never regret loving him.

After their meal, she cleaned up without complaint, but she did remind him that he would need to wash dishes for a week straight when his hand healed.

"Fair is fair," she said, her eyes twinkling.

When she joined him in the living room on the couch,

she curled against his good side, her head on his shoulder. Shane's hand stroked over her hair, which was down around her shoulders for a change.

"Are you sure?"

Kelsi nodded. "I couldn't be certainer."

He grinned, resting his forehead against hers. "Sometimes I wonder how I was so lucky as to have you for my wife, and then I remember we're both lucky, because so many people don't find real love."

"And we did. I'm never letting it go either!"

Kelsi was surprised to see Dani at the café the following morning, shortly before the lunch rush would have started. She hadn't expected to see her in the café for a few months after having to work there for three weeks. Boring banker, Fred Wharton the Third, walked into the café and slipped into the booth with her sister. Kelsi rolled her eyes. Dani was the only person she knew that he went out of his way to talk to.

Kelsi walked to the table and smiled. "What can I get for you two?" She looked back and forth between them, desperately hoping to know what was going on through the twin radar, but apparently it wasn't working that day.

Dani shrugged. "What's the soup today? I'm hearing good things about Bob's soups. And is there a new menu?"

"Normal menu is still the same. Soup is potato leek. Special is jambalaya. He set aside a small pot with extra spices just for me. He said I wouldn't be able to eat it, and I told him if he could eat one bite, I could eat a whole bowl!" Kelsi loved to prove people wrong where spices were concerned. It was yet another thing she'd inherited from Grandma Kelsey, who would always be the woman she looked up to more than any other.

Fred raised an eyebrow at her as if she was disturbing them. Kelsi rolled her eyes back at him.

"What will you have?" Her voice was as sweet as she could make it, but she wanted to poke him in the eye with a fork. She didn't trust him. *At all.*

"I'll try the jambalaya. The kind for everyone but you!" Dani said, looking at the banker.

"I'd like coke with a twist of lemon and the sirloin, medium well, with steak fries please."

"Okie dokie! I'll be back with your drinks in a minute." Kelsi hurried to the kitchen and gave Bob the order before taking the drinks out.

After she delivered them, she spotted Shane walking into the café. She hurried to him. "What are you doing here? You're not supposed to drive!" How had he gotten there? He'd better not be going against doctor's orders already!

He shrugged. "I had Bart bring me. He'll be back in an hour to pick me up."

"What happens if you're not finished in an hour?"

"He can sit in his car and wait. I'm the boss." Shane winked at her.

She laughed. "Why, Sheriff! You're in a naughty mood today."

"Soon you'll know me well enough to realize that I'm in a naughty mood every day."

Getting into the booth with him as usual, Kelsi didn't put her feet in his lap for a change. She didn't want him to think she expected him to rub her feet when he was injured. She'd wait until his arm was all better and then demand her foot rubs, like any reasonable woman would.

"How's the paperwork coming?"

He groaned. "Awful. Of course. Do you know how much I hate paperwork? I probably have three months' worth I have to do!"

"It's a good thing you hurt your left arm and not your right!" Kelsi refused to feel sorry for him. She hated paperwork as well, but she did a little every week so she wouldn't get bogged down.

"Who's the stuffed shirt with Dani?"

"I thought you knew everyone around. That's Fred Wharton the Third, he works at the bank, and he's one of Mom's spies."

"Oh! Have you heard from your mom since you told her we got married?" He hated the idea of coming between her and her mother, but he would never regret marrying her.

"Yeah, I forgot to tell you. She called yesterday while I was waiting for you to come home, and she told me that we'd find out the first part of our test this week." She rolled her eyes. "I don't want to be part of this test. It's already making me mad."

"No idea what it is? Or what this 'part' of it is?" He frowned. "I thought there was supposed to be *one* test? I guess she's doing it in pieces. Is that fair?"

"Nope. Maybe Freddy boy is over there telling Dani what we have to do."

Shane looked over his shoulder. "You really don't like him, do you?"

"I just don't like that he reports back to Mom. It makes me mad." Kelsi looked over at her sister who was leaned forward, speaking earnestly with the banker. "I wonder what they're talking about." She was quiet for a moment, trying to listen to what the other couple was saying, but they were speaking too softly.

"I'm sure Dani will tell you when they're done."

"Probably." She scooted out of the booth. "Soup today is potato leek. Special is jambalaya."

"Jambalaya sounds interesting. Is Bob going to change *everything*?"

Kelsi shrugged. "He'll still rotate in some of Grandma Kelsey's recipes, but he has some of his own too. I think he's just happy to be able to cook some of his own stuff."

"I don't like him," Shane said, knowing he sounded like a belligerent child. "I wish he hadn't come back." He didn't like that the other man got to spend all day, *every* day with Kelsi, and now he was showing off his ability to cook fancy foods. Shane could cook, but only simple things.

"Why don't you like him?" Kelsi looked toward the kitchen. "I expected to hate him, but he's really not that bad."

"He came back here to marry you!" Shane protested.

"No, he didn't. That's what Mom wanted. He was relieved I was already married before he got here."

"He told you that?"

"Yes, he did! He had no more interest in me than I had in him. He just had fond memories of the area and wanted to be in charge of his own café. I'd have come back under those circumstances as well!"

Shane didn't look convinced. "Fine, I'll eat his jambalaya." He made it sound like he was doing the other man a huge favor by eating his food.

Kelsi saw Liz and Joni come in, back from their break for the lunch rush. "You know what? I'm going to let the other waitresses handle things for a bit, and I'm going to have lunch with my husband." She rarely took a lunch break, but they were never very busy on Mondays. It would be nice to sit and eat a leisurely meal for a change.

"That sounds good to me!"

Kelsi rushed off to get the jambalaya Bob had made for her, and some of the milder version meant for Shane.

Bob followed her out. "I need to see you eat at least five bites of it!" He crossed his arms over his chest, making Shane think he wouldn't back down.

Kelsi rolled her eyes. "He thinks he made a separate pot of jambalaya too spicy for me." Nothing was too spicy for her. She kept telling him that, but he wouldn't listen.

Shane laughed softly. "She burned off all her taste buds years ago!"

Bob made a face. He carried a small spoon and stuck it into her bowl, taking one bite. His face turned red and he grabbed Kelsi's water, drinking it down. "I'll bring you more!" he choked out as he ran to refill it.

Shane watched as Bob drank two more glasses before bringing her a fresh one back. "Is this some kind of bet?"

"Of course. I get to pick who he dates if I can eat this." Kelsi grinned at Shane.

Shane laughed. "He's toast."

"Yup." She waited as Bob set the water on the table and then took a big spoonful of the jambalaya. "Not bad. Needs a little more seasoning." She looked at Bob. "Would you bring me the can of Cajun seasoning from the spice rack in the back?"

Bob raised an eyebrow but did as she asked. He watched as she poured more seasoning on the dish and then ate several bites.

"Much better," Kelsi said. When the bowl was half gone, Bob was still gaping at her. "Don't you have orders to fill?"

He walked back to the kitchen, turning periodically to look at her over his shoulder, obviously amazed anyone could eat the spicy concoction.

"What would you have had to do if you couldn't eat it?" Shane asked.

"He'd have gotten all my tips for the day!"

Shane shook his head. "He had no idea what he was up against, did he?"

Kelsi kept an eye on the table where her sister and the banker were eating, taking note when he left. She had just finished her jambalaya, and she waved Dani over.

"Any news?"

Dani nodded, rubbing her hand over her face. "Mom's going to call Wade later this week, but her first demand for our test will be to expand the kitchen and make it possible for us to have formal events here. Formal events!" Dani said, groaning as she slid into the booth beside her sister. "Where would we even *have* a formal event? We have no event halls big enough!"

"I bet that will be the second demand." Kelsi frowned at Shane. "We need to call a family meeting. Tonight. I know it's not normal for us to all get together on Mondays, but we all need to discuss this."

"We need to invite Sam as well," Dani said automatically.

"What about Wyatt? Isn't he supposed to take out a group on an overnight ride tonight?" Kelsi asked.

"Glen will have to take his place." Dani named Wyatt's right hand man, his horse-whisperer in training. Wyatt had a skill and a touch with horses that was a true gift, but Glen was proving to be an apt pupil. He had the raw talent, but he had yet to learn everything Wyatt knew.

Kelsi nodded. "I'll call everyone. Can you drop by the stables and beg Wyatt to skip his ride and come to the meeting? We *all* need to talk about this."

Dani nodded, slipping back out to stand beside the table. "How was your extra-spicy jambalaya?"

"I had to add more seasoning."

Dani rolled her eyes as she headed for the door. "Why am I not surprised?"

Shane took Kelsi's hand, squeezing it. "Expanding the kitchen for events doesn't sound like that hard of a test," he said.

Kelsi laughed. "It's hard when it's just *stage one*. Before we're done, she's going to have us building a huge event-hall, a church, and hiring a pastor. We'll have to build a carousel for the children that never come here. Probably even a mini-golf course! You watch! She's got a whole lot more in mind that some little catering operation."

"You know her better than I do."

Kelsi squeezed his hand. "Looks like Bart just drove up." She scooted out and waited until he stood, wrapping her arms around his neck and pulling his head down for a lingering kiss, despite the fact the café had been gradually filling with customers. "I love you, Sheriff Shane."

He grinned. "I'm never going to get tired of hearing you say that." He stroked his fingers over her cheek, not caring that his deputy was waiting for him.

"Good, because now I've started, I'm not sure I'm able to stop!" She watched him go, her heart full. Sure there was about to be mass chaos on the ranch, but it didn't matter. She had the man she loved by her side. Together, they could do anything.

If you've enjoyed this book, please check for more books by Kirsten Osbourne. You'll find that all the characters intertwine between series to create a huge world, connected only in her imagination.

To sign up for Kirsten Osbourne's mailing list and receive notice of new titles as they are available, click here.

Want to know more about the next book in the series? I've included a sneak peek of Pamela Kelley's Veterinarian's Vacation. Read on to learn more about Jess!

Chapter Eleven

"EARTH TO JESS?"

Jess snapped back to attention. She'd been lost in thought as she waited for a pot of coffee to finish brewing. Mr. Thomas was one of her favorite regulars and he wore an amused smile as he lifted his empty coffee cup.

"If that's done brewing, I'll take a splash," he said. He was seated at the counter and Jess brought the coffee right over to him. The breakfast rush was over and she had a tendency to forget things when it was slow. Especially today of all days.

"Here you go. It's nice and hot." She filled his cup to the rim as she knew he took it black. Jim Thomas and his buddy Fred Murphy, who was sitting on the stool next to him, were both retired and came in every morning for breakfast. They lingered over coffee as they read the paper and chatted with other customers that passed through. She topped off Fred's cup too.

"You look a little down. Everything all right?" Mr. Thomas asked.

Jess was feeling a bit blue. She always did on this date,

but he didn't need to worry about that. It was her mother's birthday and it was the only date that still made her feel sad. She'd only been eight when both her parents were killed in a car accident. Although more than seventeen years had passed she still could picture her mother's face and the blonde hair and pale blue eyes that were so like her own. She'd always had such a calm way about her and like Jess, had loved animals. She forced a smile.

"No, just busy. Thinking ahead to all the studying I need to do later."

"This is your last year, right? You'll be a true veterinarian soon?" he asked.

Jess had worked at Kelsi's Kafe for years and the customers always loved to hear updates on how school was going.

"Yes, I'm almost done. I have an internship coming up with Dr. Henery and assuming I pass all my tests, I'll be graduating this year."

"Doc Henery is getting up there. Maybe when he retires, if you play your cards right, you can take over his practice," Mr. Thomas said.

Jess laughed. "I don't want to get ahead of myself. I'll be thrilled just to get a job when I graduate."

Riston was a small town, so if she didn't get hired on permanently by Dr. Henery, there was only one other veterinarian in town and there was no guarantee that either place would be hiring. She really didn't want to have to move out of the area, but if she had to, to get a good job, she would.

The front door jingled and she turned to see her cousin Wade, walk in. Wade was her favorite of all the cousins. He was the oldest of four boys, Wyatt, Wesley and Will, and two girls, twins Kelsi and Dani. Jess loved them all. They were like the brothers and sisters she never had, especially since she'd been living with them since her parents died.

Wade was the general manager of River's End Ranch, where they all worked. Her Aunt Bobbi and Uncle Wilber used to run it, but they were unofficially retired and were touring the country in their RV, checking in from the road often to see how they were all doing or to make one of their unusual requests. The most recent had been to renovate the kitchen so that they could take on outside catering and handle larger functions at the resort.

"How's my favorite cousin?" Wade said as he came behind the counter and poured himself a cup of coffee.

"Your only cousin," she corrected him and grinned. "I'm fine. Lots of studying to do later."

Wade took a sip of coffee and then casually said, "Did I mention that I booked the Copper Cottage for the next two weeks? Possibly longer."

"Two weeks, really? Wow." People didn't usually stay that long, and the Copper Cottage was one of their nicest. It featured a chef's kitchen with a hanging copper pot rack filled with gleaming copper bottomed pots and pans. It wasn't their busiest time of the year and hadn't been rented in over a month.

"I gave it to an old friend that is going to be in town for a while. You remember Jake Wheldon?"

"Jake is coming here?" Jess found herself gripping the counter. Jake had been one of Wade's best friend's. They were the same age, thirty-two, and Jess hadn't seen Jake in a long time. And the last time she'd seen him, had been mortifying. She'd been in eighth grade and had just turned thirteen. Jake had been eighteen and was a senior in high school, about to graduate. He'd been over the house, during a crowded Christmas party, and she'd found herself standing under the mistletoe, right next to him. She'd had such a crush on Jack back then.

He was tall, dark-haired, with chocolate brown eyes and a smile that made her knees go weak. Her best friend Suzy had been there and she thought she was helping when she pointed out that they were standing under the mistletoe. Jess had been embarrassed and then thrilled, because it seemed like he was going to kiss her. She closed her eyes as he leaned forward and then cringed when he instead whispered in her ear, "I don't think this is a good idea." He gave her a quick peck on the cheek and then walked off, while Jess stood there, wanting to die. She'd avoided him after that, and after graduation, he went off to college and then veterinary school.

"I thought he was living in Lewiston now. What brings him back here?"

"Just a vacation, I think. He hasn't been back to spend any real time, other than a weekend here or there in years."

Jake's parents had divorced when he went to college and he spent his summers and school breaks with his mother, in Lewiston, so it had been a long time since even Wade had seen him.

A few minutes later, Jess was putting dirty coffee cups in the dishwasher when she heard the front door chimes jingle again. Before she could turn to look, Wade said, "There's Jake now, he said he might stop by."

Jess automatically smoothed down the flyaway hairs that always escaped from her ponytail. She knew she didn't look her best. The Kafe uniform made her feel like an awkward teenager, with its frilly apron and pink polyester. It was practical, but not overly flattering.

Wade walked out from behind the counter and gave Jake a hug and slap on the back. Jess simply tried not to stare. This Jake was a million times better looking than the high school senior she'd last seen. He still had the deep brown eyes, his hair was thick and dark and along his jaw was a faint hint of stubble. He was dressed simply in a navy button down shirt and faded jeans that fit his lean body so well. He caught her eyes and smiled.

"Jake, you remember my cousin, Jess?" Wake said. "She's studying to be a vet too."

"You were just a kid, last time I saw you," he said.

"I was thirteen, not really a kid," Jess said stiffly.

"Well, you're all grown up now. And yeah, I had heard that you're studying to be a vet."

"You did?" Jess wondered how he would have known that? Unless Wade mentioned it.

Jake smiled again and Jess couldn't help but notice how it lit up his face, how the laugh lines that danced around the corners of his mouth and eyes were so attractive.

"I have some exciting news. I just met with Doc Henery. He wants to retire and we worked out an arrangement for me to buy his practice."

"Doc Henery is retiring? When?" Jess was stunned.

"I'm taking this week off while he gets ready for me, and then I'll start with him the following week. He also mentioned that you're going to be starting an internship there…so, I guess that makes me your new boss."

About the Author

www.kirstenandmorganna.com

Made in the USA
Monee, IL
13 January 2022

88822657R00095